THE

SLITHER

SISTERS

THE SLITHER SISTERS

TALES FROM

LOVECRAFT MIDDLE SCHOOL #2

By
CHARLES GILMAN

Illustrations by
EUGENE SMITH

QUIRK BOOKS

PHILADELPHIA

Library of Congress Cataloging in Publication Number: 2011946054

ISBN: 978-1-59474-593-5
Printed in China
Typeset in Bembo, House Monster Fonts, and Melior

Designed by Doogie Horner
Cover photography by Jonathan Pushnik
Cover models: Evangeline Young, Audrey Coughenour, and Damien
Production management by John J. McGurk
Lenticular manufactured by National Graphics, Inc.

Quirk Books
215 Church Street
Philadelphia, PA 19106
quirkbooks.com

10 9 8 7 6 5 4 3 2 1

This book
is for Anna

ONE

Robert Arthur and Glenn Torkells were sitting in the principal's office.

School had ended twenty minutes earlier. Their classmates were on the lush green lawns of Lovecraft Middle School, tossing Frisbees and baseballs, getting on bikes, and heading for home.

But Robert and Glenn weren't going anywhere.

They had an appointment to see Principal Slater.

The only other person in the office was the principal's secretary, Mrs. Polyps. Her fingers pecked frantically at her computer keyboard. Every few moments, she glanced over at the boys and smiled. Her teeth were the color of a yellow school bus.

"This is a dumb idea," Glenn whispered.

"Shhh," Robert said.

"No one *chooses* to go to the principal's office," Glenn continued. "You avoid this place. You don't *volunteer* to come here and hang out."

"We're not hanging out," Robert said. "We're going to tell her the school is in danger."

"She'll think you're bonkers."

"I can prove it."

Glenn snorted. "I'd like to see how you prove that an army of monsters is getting ready to attack Lovecraft Middle School."

Mrs. Polyps abruptly stopped typing.

"Be quiet," Robert whispered.

"Dumb idea," Glenn repeated. "You'll see."

Underneath Robert's chair, his backpack squirmed. Inside were his pets, a two-headed rat named Pip and Squeak. They had snuck into his backpack a few weeks earlier and they insisted on accompanying him wherever he went. Robert tapped the backpack with his sneaker until the rats fell still.

The boys waited nearly half an hour before Principal Slater opened her door. There were rumors going around Lovecraft Middle School that she used to work as an actress on daytime soap operas. Robert didn't know if the stories were true, but they were easy enough to believe. Principal Slater was very pretty and had a warm, inviting smile. "I'm sorry to keep you waiting," she said. "Come on back."

She ushered them into a sunny office lined with awards and certificates. On her desk were framed photographs of family members and pets. She sat across from Robert and Glenn and sipped coffee from a mug that read WORLD'S BEST PRINCIPAL.

"How can I help you?"

"There's something we need to explain," Robert said, "but it's gonna sound a little weird."

"*A lot* weird," Glenn corrected.

"Go on," she said, taking another sip.

"We know who kidnapped Sarah and Sylvia Price."

Principal Slater dropped her mug, spilling coffee all over her desk. She didn't bother to clean it up. She

9

didn't even seem to notice.

"This better not be a joke," she warned.

"I wish I was kidding," Robert said.

The disappearance of Sarah and Sylvia Price, seventh-grade twins at Lovecraft Middle School, had made headlines throughout New England. Parents feared that the girls had been abducted by some kind of psycho predator. Police led searches through all the surrounding forests, parks, and cities. They found nothing—no evidence, no leads, no clues.

Then, just five days later, Sarah and Sylvia mysteriously returned home, seemingly unharmed, with no memory of where they had been or who had taken them. The police department was baffled. The neighborhood was outraged. But the girls insisted that there was nothing to worry about, everything was fine. They just wanted to go back to living their lives.

"I'm going to call the police," Principal Slater explained, "and we're going to talk about this with some detectives. But first I want you to tell me who kidnapped Sarah and Sylvia."

"This is the weird part," Glenn warned.

Robert nodded. "They were kidnapped by monsters."

Principal Slater leaned forward. "Could you say that last part again? It sounded like you said 'monsters.'"

Robert took a deep breath and started from the beginning. He reminded her that Lovecraft Middle School had been constructed almost entirely from recycled materials—old windows, doors, floor tiles, and the like. What most people didn't realize is that these materials had come from an abandoned mansion on the far end of town. Thirty years ago, this mansion had been home to a physicist named Crawford Tillinghast. He had been working in secret with a team of scientists to summon ancient races of demons and monsters. It was widely believed that Tillinghast and his employees had died in an explosion, but the truth was more complicated.

"They didn't really die," Robert explained. "They just copied the house to another dimension."

"Another dimension," Principal Slater repeated. "I

don't know what that means."

"Like a world within our world," Robert explained. "And here's the really crazy part. When the original mansion was recycled into Lovecraft Middle School, it created these holes. Like gates between the two worlds. If you find one, you can leave Lovecraft Middle School and cross over to Tillinghast Mansion."

"Have you done this yourself?" Principal Slater asked. "You've been inside this Tillyghost Mansion?"

"Tillinghast," Glenn corrected.

"We've been there," Robert said. "So have Sarah and Sylvia Price. That's what we're trying to explain. They crossed over to Tillinghast and their souls were captured. The girls who returned aren't really Sarah and Sylvia. They're monsters in disguise."

Principal Slater shook her head in weary disbelief. "Seriously? Like Frankenstein?"

"More prehistoric," Robert said. "Like ancient demons. They wear our skins like masks."

Principal Slater laughed. "Come on, boys. You're talking to a former biology teacher. Do you understand how the human epidermis works? Do you understand why this is anatomically impossible?"

"I know it sounds crazy," Robert said. "But I've seen it. We both have."

"It's true," Glenn said. "Professor Goyle was one of them. And now they've got Sarah and Sylvia Price."

Principal Slater brought both hands to her head, as if trying to steady her thoughts. "Let's assume everything you're saying is true. What would you like me to do?"

"Tell people," Robert said. "Tell everyone. Before any more kids are captured."

"I can't tell this story without proof," Principal Slater said. "People will think I'm nuts. What kind of evidence do you have?"

Robert shook his head. "Nothing."

"Nothing? No photos on a cell phone? No witnesses? Nothing at home in your bedroom?"

"Not yet," Robert admitted.

"We're working on it," Glenn said.

"That's not good enough." Principal Slater rose

from her desk, walked over to the door, and punched a passcode into the lock. The deadbolt turned with a loud *thunk*. "Without proof, I'm afraid can't tell anyone."

When she returned to her chair, Robert saw that her face was flushed. Something was wrong. The skin on her forehead was twitching, pulsing, *blistering*. Principal Slater continued speaking like nothing was out of the ordinary, but her voice had deepened to a hoarse croak: "I'm afraid we'll have to keep this just between us."

She extended her left arm, only it wasn't an arm, not anymore—it was a slender, slippery tentacle covered with hundreds of tiny suckers.

Glenn recoiled but wasn't fast enough. Principal Slater already had him by the waist. Another tentacle lashed out, coiling around his leg and hoisting him out of his chair.

Robert yanked the tentacle by its tip, trying to wrest it loose, only to find the surface covered in barbed stingers; it was like squeezing a handful of thorns.

"Grab my ankles!" Glenn shouted.

Robert tried but wasn't strong enough to hold on. By this point Principal Slater had molted the rest of her human skin; she now resembled something like a giant frog with an enormous mouth. She was still speaking, but her language was incomprehensible: "*Zlagh fahn mynakos. Zlagh f'yaloh!*"

She didn't stop speaking until she had stuffed Glenn's head and torso into her gaping maw. His legs flailed back and forth as gravity forced him further down the creature's throat.

Robert climbed onto the principal's desk and pulled on Glenn's feet, but his puny arms were no match for the giant slurping jaws of the beast. Robert was too weak to do anything. He was too weak, too weak, too weak . . .

CHAPTER

TWO

Then the door opened.

And everything changed.

No Glenn. No principal. No frog monster.

Just Mrs. Arthur, Robert's mother, dressed in her nurse's scrubs, standing in the doorway of his bedroom with one hand on the light switch.

"Sweetie?" she asked. "Are you all right?"

Robert sat up in bed. He'd been having a nightmare. Just the latest in a long string of nightmares since he'd arrived at Lovecraft Middle School six weeks ago.

"I'm fine," he said. "Just a bad dream."

"Go back to sleep."

His mother turned off the light and closed the

door. Robert glanced over at his clock radio. It was still early, not even six o'clock, but he knew he wouldn't fall back asleep.

He walked downstairs to the kitchen, where his mother was eating a bowl of cornflakes and clipping coupons from the newspaper. Mrs. Arthur worked the early shift at Dunwich Memorial Hospital; most mornings, she was out the door before Robert woke up.

"You want me to fix you some eggs?"

"No, thanks."

"You're sure? I've got time."

"I'm not hungry."

Mrs. Arthur frowned. "What was your dream about?"

Robert wished he could tell his mother the truth, but he didn't want her to worry. She already had enough problems, between doing all the cooking and all the cleaning and earning enough money to support them. She didn't need to know that his school was full of portals to an alternate dimension.

"I don't remember," he finally said.

She could tell he was lying. "You can talk to me," she assured him. "What's going on?"

He shrugged. "I'm not sure how to explain it."

Mrs. Arthur abruptly stood up and left the kitchen. She returned moments later with a brown cardboard shoe box. "I was going to save this for your birthday, but I want you to have it now."

"What is it?"

"Open it," she said. "Go on."

Robert pulled off the lid. Inside he found a hairbrush, two sticks of roll-on deodorant, a pack of disposable razors, and a can of shaving cream.

"It's a Puberty Kit," his mother explained.

"A what?"

"Your body's changing, Robert. It's a very stressful time. These are the tools you'll need as you grow into a man."

Robert already knew all about puberty. At school, they'd been warning him about puberty since the fourth grade.

"This is a confusing time to be a boy, and it's normal

to have worries," his mother continued. "I just wish you had a father to answer your personal questions."

Robert sifted through the contents of the Puberty Kit. At the bottom of the box was a paperback book called *Help! My Body Is Changing!* On the cover was an illustration of a nervous-looking twelve-year-old boy with question marks exploding from his head.

"If you have something you don't feel comfortable asking me," his mother explained, "you might find the answer inside this book. Remember, you can't trust what you read on the Internet."

"I know," Robert said. "Thank you."

After his mother left for work, he read the book's table of contents. It consisted of one hundred short cries for help:

> Help! My Voice Is Changing!
> Help! My Armpits Are Stinky!
> Help! I'm Getting Pimples!

Robert closed the book and sighed.

The truth—and he'd rather die than admit the truth to anyone—was that he didn't have any of these problems. His voice *wasn't* changing. His armpits *weren't* stinky. He'd *almost* had a pimple, but it turned out to be a mosquito bite.

Meanwhile, all the other kids in his grade were growing up fast. Glenn was just three months older than Robert, but he'd already been shaving for a year. The other boys in their class were getting taller and stronger and faster and louder; compared to them Robert still looked and felt like a little kid.

He scanned the page looking for an entry that read "Help! I'm Almost Thirteen Years Old and I Still Have the Muscles of a Third-Grader!" but apparently Robert's condition was so freakish and rare, the authors of the book didn't even bother to include it.

Pip and Squeak climbed onto his shoulder and nuzzled his neck, hungry for their breakfast. Robert scratched them behind the ears. "Well," he said, "it's a good thing we have more important things to worry about."

CHAPTER

THREE

Later that morning, when Robert arrived at school, the main lobby was filled with seventh- and eighth-graders. There appeared to be some kind of pep rally. Robert was greeted by a girl carrying a tray of cupcakes.

"Success has a price!" she exclaimed, pushing a cupcake into his hands. "Vote Sarah Price!"

There were muffins and brownies and cookies, too—all arranged on a table festooned with balloons and streamers. Sarah and Sylvia Price were chatting and laughing and dishing out treats. The PA system was blasting pop songs. Robert had never been to a real teenage party with music and dancing, but he imag-

ined this was what they looked like.

Sarah climbed onto a chair and shouted, "Lovecraft students are the best! I love you guys!"

"We love you too, Sarah!" someone shouted back.

"I love my sister!" Sylvia exclaimed. "Go Sarah! You're awesome! Go Lovecraft! Wooooo!"

Robert pushed his way through the crowd. He

found Glenn Torkells and Karina Ortiz watching from a distance, far from the other students.

"What the heck is going on?" he asked.

"Sarah's running for student council president," Glenn said.

"Why?"

"It's a smart move," Karina said. "Tillinghast wants to take over the school, so he's starting at the top. Once Sarah controls student council, she can lead all the students right into his trap."

Karina was Robert's only other friend at Lovecraft Middle School—and the only other person who knew the secret of the Price sisters. Karina had died in Tillinghast Mansion at the age of twelve and her spirit was imprisoned behind its walls for thirty years. Robert and Glenn helped her escape to Lovecraft Middle School, where she passed herself off as a living, breathing middle school student. You'd never know she was a ghost unless you accidentally bumped into her—which is why Karina always lingered on the edges of crowds, far from the other students.

"Do you think she'll win?" Robert asked.

"Of course she will. She's pretty and popular and all her friends are going to vote for her."

Sarah certainly had tons of friends, judging from the crowds in the hallway. "Who's running against her?"

"I forget his name," Glenn said. "Harold somebody."

He pointed to a boy sitting alone at an empty table, holding a mug full of No. 2 pencils. This was Howard Mergler, a boy from Robert's Social Studies class. Howard had been in a car accident three years earlier, and now he walked using forearm crutches and wore orthotic braces on his knees. If you got stuck behind him walking down a flight of stairs, you were guaranteed to be late for class.

"Hey, Howard," Robert said.

"Good morning!" Howard held out the mug. "Would you like a pencil?"

"Sure."

"Sharpened or unsharpened?"

"Um, I don't care."

Howard gave him one of each. The pencils were

inscribed with the words FOR SMART & RESPONSIBLE
LEADERSHIP VOTE HOWARD MER.

"Howard Mer?" Robert asked.

"There was only space for fifty characters," Howard
sighed. "No one told me when I placed the order. I
should have just made cupcakes."

"Who wants cupcakes?" Sarah shouted.

"Who wants brownies?" Sylvia cheered.

"Wooooooooooo!" they hollered together.

Howard ignored them. "If I'm elected president,"
he promised Robert, "I'll keep school computers at the
forefront of technology. And I'll bring more nutritious
lunches into the school cafeteria . . ."

Someone cranked up the dance music. A pounding
bass shook the metal doors of the lockers: *thump, thump,
thump-thump-thump.* Robert couldn't hear a word
Howard was saying, but he realized the words didn't
matter.

In an election against Sarah Price, a candidate like
Howard Mergler didn't stand a chance.

CHAPTER

FOUR

In the days to come, the halls of Lovecraft Middle School were filled with posters advertising Sarah's campaign. They all featured the same phrase: SUCCESS COMES WITH A PRICE. It was meant to be a snappy campaign slogan—but to Robert the words sounded like a warning: *If Sarah won the election, there would literally be hell to pay.*

But who would believe him?

How could he warn people?

What proof did he have?

The Price sisters looked like perfectly normal, all-American girls. They had photographs of boy bands taped inside their lockers. Their grades were good but not suspiciously good; they earned B's and B-pluses on every quiz, test, and book report. Sarah played the violin; Sylvia played field hockey. They both contributed moody poetry to the school's literary magazine.

They behaved like all the other seventh-grade girls at Lovecraft Middle School in every way except one:

They never ate lunch.

Every day at eleven forty-five, when the bell rang and hundreds of seventh-graders filed into the cafeteria, Sarah and Sylvia were nowhere to be found.

Karina explained that they were probably revolted by the flavors of human food. "The creatures at Tillinghast prefer live meat. They'll eat anything as long as it's breathing. Rodents, birds, amphibians. Even bugs."

Robert imagined the Price sisters sharing a bowl of live crickets in the middle of the school cafeteria. No wonder they were dining in secret.

"We need to find them," he said. "They're up to something, and we need to know what it is."

That became his mission. Every day during lunch period, Robert wolfed down his sandwich and then wandered the hallways of the school, hoping to catch the Price sisters eating roaches in the gym or the computer lab or the music room. It was hard to do so without arousing the attention of his teachers. While searching the library, he was repeatedly approached by Ms. Lavinia, the elderly school librarian.

"Can I help you, Mr. Arthur?"

"No, thanks."

"Are you looking for something in particular?"

"I'm just browsing."

The library was a labyrinth of tall shelves that offered plenty of places for Sarah and Sylvia to hide; as Robert wandered its corridors, Ms. Lavinia was always close by, alphabetizing books or pushing a rickety wooden cart with a squeaky wheel.

Glenn helped search, too. While Robert explored the inside of the school, Glenn scoped out the tennis courts, the athletic stadium, the parking lots, and the picnic areas. It was a funny thing: there was a time when Robert and Glenn couldn't stand each other. Glenn had a reputation as the biggest bully in Dunwich,

Massachusetts, and he had picked on Robert for years. But after Robert saved Glenn from a squid-monster, the two boys had joined forces, and they were unlikely friends ever since.

After three days of searching the school for Sarah and Sylvia, it was Karina who finally discovered where the sisters were hiding during lunch.

"The swimming pool!" she exclaimed. The lunch bell had just rung, and she stopped Robert and Glenn in the hallway outside the cafeteria. "They're in the girls' locker room," she said, "changing into swimsuits. We need to go right now!"

Robert had been hearing about Lovecraft's amazing swimming pool since the first day of classes but had yet to see it firsthand; he'd never been able to find it. Karina led them into the east wing and down a stairwell, and soon Robert was completely disoriented. "Where are you taking us?" he asked.

"This is it," Karina announced.

She had stopped in front of a door labeled THE WILBUR WHATELEY MEMORIAL NATATORIUM.

"What about the pool?" he asked.

"This *is* the pool," Karina explained. "A natatorium is a room with a pool inside it."

Glenn opened the door. "Holy cow."

It was the biggest indoor swimming pool they had ever seen, fifty meters long and up to twelve feet deep. There were ten lanes for swimming and three platforms for diving.

But no sign of Sarah or Sylvia Price.

"They'll be here any second," Karina said.

"We should hide," Glenn said.

Robert looked around for a good place but didn't see one. The air in the natatorium tickled the back of his throat. It was warm and humid and reeked of chlorine.

"Over here," Karina called.

Spanning the length of the pool were rows of metal bleachers for coaches, parents, and other spectators. Karina had already climbed behind the stands. It was a tight squeeze for Robert and even worse for Glenn; they had to crouch down on all fours to fit through.

"What if a teacher catches us?" Glenn asked.

"Don't worry," Karina said. "As long as we don't move, no one's going to see us."

It was true: to anyone looking at the bleachers, the kids were virtually invisible, camouflaged by the benches and rails and supports.

From their hiding place, Robert could see only the very surface of the water, as clear and still as glass. Time creeped forward.

"You're sure they were in the locker room?" he asked.

Karina nodded. "They're coming here every day. The question is, why?"

Robert wasn't sure he wanted to know the answer. The last time he tried spying on someone, he'd witnessed his Science teacher, Professor Goyle, eating a live hamster.

Moments later, Sarah and Sylvia emerged from the locker room, dressed in simple one-piece swimsuits and chatting pleasantly. To anyone watching, they appeared to be perfectly ordinary sisters. But to anyone listening, they sounded like snorting, snarling lunatics.

"*Yh'nghai tsathogua dho-na,*" said Sarah.

Sylvia smiled. "*Y'golonac chaugnar faugn.*"

"*Hgulet tcho-tcho, ep hgulut shaggai.*"

It was the same bizarre language that Professor Goyle had spoken—but what did it mean? Robert had no idea.

The sisters had reached the edge of the pool and were preparing to dive in when Sylvia stopped, scowled, and raised her hand. "*Gnai glaacki!*"

Both girls glanced around the natatorium, as if suddenly realizing they weren't alone.

Together, they approached the bleachers.

A long forked tongue unfurled from Sarah's mouth, purple and black and eight inches long. It flicked this way and that, dripping with saliva. Robert remembered learning in Science class that certain reptiles used their tongues to detect smell. He forced himself to remain absolutely still, hoping all the chlorine in the natatorium would mask his scent.

Then he felt something shift inside his backpack.

Pip and Squeak spent most mornings napping but usually woke around noon for lunch—and they never hesitated to let Robert know when they were hungry. He closed his eyes, wishing they would sleep for just a few moments longer. *Take it easy, guys,* he thought. *Stay still for one more minute.* And immediately the rats stopped wiggling, as if they had somehow read his mind.

Finally, Sarah retracted her tongue, satisfied they were alone.

"*Shai shabblat?*" Sylvia asked.

"*Y'ai zhro,*" Sarah replied.

Together they raised their arms above their heads and then dove into the deep end. Robert watched the water lapping against the edges of the pool, the waves slowly ebbing until once again the surface was as clear and still as glass.

"What are they doing?" Glenn whispered.

"Shhh," Robert said.

He was counting off the seconds—forty-one, forty-two, forty-three—wondering how long Sarah and Sylvia could stay underwater before surfacing for air.

Robert counted all the way to three hundred before stopping.

"How long can you hold your breath?" he whispered to Glenn.

"I don't know. Maybe a minute? They've been down there for five."

"They're not human," Karina reminded them. "Some creatures can stay underwater for hours."

"Right," Robert said. "But why? What are they doing down there?"

No one could answer that question.

"We need to see what they're up to," he said. "There has to be a reason they come here every day."

Robert squeezed out from behind the bleachers and crept toward the pool. He wanted to glimpse the sisters without being seen—but they remained just out of view. He had no choice but to step right up to the edge of the water.

"Glenn? Karina?" he called. "You can come out."

His friends rushed to his side and looked down into the pool. Apart from several hundred thousand gallons of water, it was empty.

"What happened?" Glenn asked.

"They vanished," Robert said.

Karina shook her head. "They crossed over," she said. "There must be a gate at the bottom."

Robert realized she was right. This would explain why Sarah and Sylvia returned to the pool every day: they were traveling back and forth between Lovecraft Middle School and Tillinghast Mansion.

He sat down at the edge of the pool, unlaced his sneakers, and pulled off his socks.

Glenn knelt beside him. "What are you doing?"

"We have to hurry," Robert said. "They've got a five-minute head start."

CHAPTER

FIVE

"You're crazy!" Glenn said. "You want to follow them?"

"I want to try," Robert said. "Before the gate closes. Let's see if we can cross over."

"You don't even know how to swim!" Glenn exclaimed.

Technically, this wasn't true. Robert could swim but had never learned how to swim *properly*, so his arms and legs tired quickly. But that wouldn't be an issue this morning. "It's just ten feet to the bottom," he said. "Anyone can sink ten feet."

"What about a bathing suit?"

"There's no time to change."

Robert stashed his backpack behind the bleachers. Pip and Squeak were still waking up, and he ordered them to sit tight. "We'll get lunch when I'm back," he explained.

Then he jumped into the pool, jeans and sweatshirt and all. As his clothes soaked up water, it felt like he had gained an extra twenty pounds of body weight.

Glenn yanked off his boots and tossed them under the bleachers. "I've been meaning to wash these clothes, anyway," he said. "You coming, Karina?"

"Of course," she shrugged. "You guys wouldn't last five minutes on the other side without me."

Glenn cannonballed into the pool, splashing giant waves over the sides. But Karina dove into the water without making a splash or even a ripple. It was one of the weirdest things Robert had ever seen: instead of swimming *in* the water, she was somehow swimming *between* it. And when she rose to the surface, her face and hair were completely dry.

"Everybody ready?" Robert asked.

"Let's go," Glenn said.

Karina nodded. "Last one to the gate is a rotten egg!"

She plunged beneath the water, leading the way, down, down, down to the bottom of the pool. Glenn followed, then Robert. The extra weight of their clothes helped them sink quickly.

Robert descended headfirst, searching the bottom of the pool for signs of a gate. On dry land, they were easy to recognize—whirling vortexes that hovered in the air. Underwater, they were proving harder to spot. Underwater, *everything* was whirling.

Soon Robert realized he had a bigger problem. The pool was supposed to have a maximum depth of ten feet. Karina and Glenn and Robert should have reached bottom in a few seconds, but somehow the tiled floor remained just a few inches beyond their fingertips. They seemed to be going lower and lower without getting anywhere.

When Robert finally paused to look up, he realized they had descended into a sort of canyon. The sunlit surface of the pool was now fifty feet above—and

he was still sinking. The water was turning darker and darker.

Robert wanted to call out to his friends and make them stop. Going deeper seemed like a terrible idea. What if the pool had no bottom? What if it stretched into infinity?

But turning back wasn't an option. Robert tried but found his clothes were too heavy; his arms and legs were too weak. The best he could manage was treading water—keeping himself from falling farther. He paddled his arms and legs, venting bubbles through his nose, wasting precious energy and air. His muscles were going numb. His lungs were nearly empty.

"Guys!" he yelled. Underwater the word was just a muffled noise. Glenn and Karina didn't look back, and Robert realized he had made an incredibly stupid mistake. The silent scream had depleted the last of his air, and the edges of his vision were blurring. He was now seconds away from drowning.

He reached toward his friends, wishing they would turn around, wishing they would see he needed help.

And then Karina disappeared into darkness.

But, no—Robert could still see the wall beyond her. Somehow she had vanished *through* the wall.

She had found the gate!

A moment later, Glenn disappeared, too.

Robert summoned the last of his energy, forcing his exhausted muscles to work just a little harder. There was a pressure in the gate that drew him in, flushing his body through to the next dimension. In an instant, the water turned from dark black to sunny bright green, and Robert suddenly realized he could stand.

His head broke the surface of the water and Robert choked on his first gasp of air. He opened his eyes but couldn't see; his face was covered with some sort of muck. He flailed about in the water, coughing and wheezing, until Glenn scooped one arm under his shoulder, holding him steady.

"Take it easy," he said. "Just breathe."

Robert rinsed the muck away from his eyes. He and Glenn were standing up to their necks in a small outdoor pond. Glenn's hair, face, and shoulders were covered with slime. Floating on the surface of the water was a fuzzy carpet of bright green algae. Robert could feel the stuff in his hair, in his ears, on his lips. He spat several times into the water. "This is disgusting!"

"Don't blame me," Glenn said. "This was your idea."

Together they trudged to the edge of the pond. In front of them was a large four-story home. Robert recognized it from newspaper photographs as the Tillinghast Mansion. Even though they had crossed into another dimension that was some thirty years earlier, the time of day hadn't changed. The sun was directly overhead. It couldn't have been much past noon.

Karina was already out of the pond, crouching behind some shrubbery. Somehow she was still dry—she'd swum through the water without getting wet. "Come over here," she said. "Before someone sees you." Robert crawled out onto the grass, covered in slime, and collapsed. Karina wrinkled her nose. "You smell awful."

"I feel awful," he said.

"We'll rest a few minutes," Glenn said. "Give you a chance to catch your breath. Then we'll go back."

"Back?"

"Through the water."

Robert shook his head. Swimming down through the pool had been hard enough. But swimming up? "I can't. We have to find a different gate."

Glenn laughed. "How are we going to do that? You want to knock on the door and ask Tillinghast for help?"

Robert studied the mansion, searching the windows for signs of life: Nothing. No faces in the windows. No cars in the driveway. And certainly no sign of Sarah or Sylvia Price. The place appeared deserted.

"Maybe no one's here," Robert whispered.

"Someone's always here," Karina said.

"Someone's *definitely* here," Glenn said. "When I look at this house, I can feel it looking back at me."

They spent the next few minutes debating their options. Glenn insisted on going back in the water. He said it was only a matter of time before someone—or some*thing*—from the mansion spotted them. And tried to eat them. "Do you remember the giant spider?" he asked.

"I remember," Robert said. The last time they sneaked into Tillinghast Mansion, they were nearly eaten by an enormous hungry spider and thousands of her spiderlings.

But as much as Robert hated giant bugs, he was even more afraid about going back into the water. He'd just come within moments of drowning and he was still dripping wet. He would rather take his chances inside the house.

"Let's just peek through the windows," Robert said. "Maybe we'll see a gate."

"That's pretty unlikely," Glenn said, turning to Karina. "Isn't it?"

They both looked to Karina to make the decision. As often happened, she would have the tiebreaking vote. She stood up and walked toward the front door. "We've come this far, we might as well take a peek."

"Wait for me," Robert said.

"Fine," Glenn said, scrambling after them, "but if we see one spiderweb I'm jumping back in this water and leaving you here."

CHAPTER SIX

As they followed the walkway to the front door of the mansion, Robert realized the yard was completely silent. There were no sounds of cars from neighboring streets, no lawn mowers or leaf blowers buzzing in the distance. Even the wind had fallen silent.

The grounds of the mansion were deathly still.

There were two large windows beside the front door, but these were blocked by tangles of tall thorny vines. Robert tried pushing them back and immediately pricked his finger. He studied one of the windows from a distance. The drapes were open but the glass was covered with a thick layer of grime, making it difficult to see anything inside. Yet he recognized a familiar shape.

"Look!" he told Glenn, pointing.

There, just inside the house, was a swirling black vortex.

"I don't believe it," Glenn said. "You were right!"

As Robert and Glenn stepped aside, Karina peered through the window and frowned. "Guys, wait. That's not what you think—"

But it was too late. Robert and Glenn were already opening the massive front door and stepping into the entrance hall.

It was the sort of space that was common in old houses, with a large stone hearth, a spectacular glass chandelier, and a grand staircase leading to the second floor.

Yet the hall's most impressive features were its magnificent tapestries. There were six in all, enormous woven portraits that stretched all the way to the ceiling. One showed a giant pyramid with an eyeball floating above it, like the picture on the back of a dollar bill, except this pyramid was surrounded by men and women dressed in red tunics, like ancient Romans.

Another tapestry showed a large black vortex at

the peak of a mountain, with swarms of children ascending the mountain to reach it. With a sinking feeling, Robert realized this was the gate he'd seen through the window—not a real gate at all. "It's just a painting," he said.

Karina scowled. "If you'd listened to me, you would know that already. Have you forgotten that I spent thirty years trapped in this house? I know my way around."

"You can give us a tour some other time," Glenn said. "I'm going to back to the water."

Glenn was still speaking as the hinges squealed behind him. The wooden door closed with a crash that rocked the chandelier and shook the rest of the house. He hurried over to open it, only to find that there were no doorknobs, latches, or handles. Just an enormous slab of mahogany wood.

"What is this?" Glenn asked. "How are people supposed to open this?"

"They're not," Karina said. "That's the point. Getting *in* the house is easy. Leaving is a different story." Footsteps sounded overhead and Karina looked up to the ceiling. "And here come our hosts."

Robert looked around the hall. There were some chairs and a table beside the hearth but no real place to hide, and certainly nothing that could be used as a weapon.

"I'll break the windows," Glenn said.

Desperate, he lifted a chair off the floor, as if preparing to fling it through the glass.

Then he froze.

Sarah and Sylvia were standing at the top of the stairs. They were dressed in matching crimson gowns. Just like the tunics worn by the men and women in the tapestry.

Robert braced himself, preparing for the worst.

He expected horns to sprout from their heads. Or wings to burst from their backs. Or giant tongues to emerge from their mouths.

He expected the girls to come charging down the stairs, claws extended, shrieking and screaming.

He certainly didn't expect them to *smile*.

"Karina!" they exclaimed together.

"Master will be so excited to learn you've come home!" Sarah said. "And you've brought boys!"

"We need more boys!" Sylvia said. "Have they come to surrender their vessels?"

Karina blinked. "Yes. That's right."

"Wonderful!" Sarah said, clapping her hands.

"Master will be very pleased!" Sylvia agreed.

The sisters bounded down the stairs, overjoyed to be welcoming guests.

Glenn glanced about anxiously. "What do they mean, 'surrender their vessels'?" he whispered. "What are they talking about?"

"Shhhh," Karina whispered back. "Just play along."

Sarah took Robert by the hand, leading him into the hall. "You poor thing, you're dripping wet." She produced a towel out of nowhere and dabbed the slime from Robert's face and hair. "How about a cup of tea? Something to warm you up? We were just about to have lunch."

"Let's sit by the fire," Sylvia agreed. She was fussing over Glenn, picking bits of algae from his hair and tossing them over her shoulder. "You'll be warm and toasty in no time."

Robert and Glenn hesitated. The Price sisters were being so friendly, it was easy to forget they had eight-inch tongues tucked behind their smiles.

"Great idea," Karina said. "Come on, guys."

The sisters spread blankets across the sofa and invited the boys to sit facing the fire. Karina sat between them. The hall's largest tapestry was directly above the hearth. It portrayed an enormous human arm growing out of a desert landscape, its massive fingers reaching toward a blazing red sky.

The sisters sat in chairs on either side of the sofa.

Sarah smiled. "You boys must be so excited."

Robert and Glenn stared back at her. What were they supposed to say?

"Yes," Karina answered. "They're very excited."

"It's normal to be nervous," Sarah continued, "but I assure you, boys, the surrender is completely painless."

"After the first decade," Sylvia quickly added.

"That's right," said Sarah. "Some complain for a few

years, but eventually everyone quiets down and then it's smooth sailing for centuries. And what an opportunity! To serve the Great Old Ones in this way—it's really quite an honor."

Glenn glanced around, thoroughly confused. "What do you mean, 'serve the Great Old Ones'?"

"By surrendering your bodies! Those useless slabs of skin and hair and gristle! They allow us to walk among your peers unnoticed."

"What happens to us?" Robert asked.

"Oh, don't worry," Sarah said. "We have a very nice room for you downstairs."

"It's more of an urn," Sylvia corrected.

"A small, urn-shaped room," Sarah said. "You'll be so comfortable, you'll never want to leave."

"Even if you could," Sylvia said.

"You must be so proud!"

Robert tried to put it all together. "You're going to use our bodies as disguises? While we live inside jars?"

"You're pioneers!" Sarah exclaimed. "We'll possess all your classmates eventually. But you boys are among the first. Master will remember your allegiance when the Great War is over."

"Hear, hear," Sylvia cheered. "Let's have some tea."

She reached for a handbell on the end table and gave it four distinct rings. Robert glanced around the hall, desperate to find some way out of their predicament. The front door was inoperable. He had Price sisters flanking him. Even if he could get past them, he had no idea where to go . . .

A door swung open and in walked a stoop-backed elderly woman. She carried an ancient wicker tray with a ceramic teapot and four small cups. As she arranged the cups on the table, Robert recognized her as Ms. Lavinia—the suspicious librarian with the rickety wooden cart. But she gave no indication of recognizing Robert or Glenn.

"Thank you, Claudine," Sarah said. "Serve the gentlemen first, please."

"As you wish," she whispered.

She carried the teapot around the table, filling the cups with an oily black sludge. It smelled like a mix of diesel fuel and the swamp they'd just come through.

"What kind of tea is this?" Glenn asked.

"Larval," Sylvia replied. "We brew it in the greenhouse."

Robert peered into his cup. Floating on the surface and staring back at him was a bulbous head with a long, skinny tail. A giant tadpole.

Sylvia reached into her cup, plucked a tadpole by its tail, and popped it into her mouth like a maraschino cherry. She chewed slowly, savoring the flavors, and Robert could hear bones crunching in her mouth. "Mmmmm," she said, raising her cup. "More, Claudine."

As Ms. Lavinia leaned over to fill the cup, her hand shook, and a drop of tea splashed onto Sarah's gown. She shrieked and leapt from her chair. "Stupid mammal!"

"Forgive me!" Ms. Lavinia exclaimed, stumbling backward and losing her grip on the wicker tray. It fell with the teapot into the hearth and flames billowed out, rising above the mantel and igniting the bottom of the tapestry. Sarah moved to swat the flames with a towel but an oblivious Ms. Lavinia was blocking her way, offering apologies and pleading for forgiveness.

"Move, you useless bag of bones!" Sarah shrieked. "Before the whole house burns!"

Robert felt a tug on his wrist and realized that Glenn and Karina were already off the sofa. He scrambled after them.

"Which way?" he asked.

"Doesn't matter," Karina said. "Go!"

Glenn threw open the nearest door and they found themselves in a short corridor with four additional doors. Glenn chose the closest, and this time they emerged in a large kitchen with dozens of cupboards and cabinets. Robert rushed to the door leading outside, but again it had no locks or handles; there was no way to open it.

"Get in a cabinet," Glenn said.

"No way," Robert said. "We'll be sitting ducks."

"We have like five seconds to hide," Karina said. "Any moment now they're going to come charging through that door."

On a countertop in the center of the kitchen was a tall steel pot with a cinder block balanced across its lid. Robert couldn't understand why anyone would keep a cinder block in the kitchen—until he heard the scratching.

Something was *inside* the pot. Clawing at its sides.

Robert reached for the cinder block.

"What are you doing?" Glenn asked. "There's no time!"

"But it's trapped," Robert said. "We can't leave it—"

He had barely lifted the cinder block when the lid clattered to the floor and a sopping wet cat sprang out, bolting across the kitchen and vanishing down the hallway, leaving a trail of foul sludge across the floor. The stench was disgusting.

"It's a marinade," Karina explained. "I don't know how they can stomach it."

The kitchen door burst open and in came Ms. Lavinia, her face flushed and her dress smeared with soot.

"You stupid, stupid children," she said. "You need to leave. Immediately!"

Ms. Lavinia reached for the handle of the nearest cupboard—only to reveal it wasn't a cupboard at all. It appeared to be a window into a tall, vertical well—a sort of miniature elevator shaft, running straight down the center of the building.

"Get in," she said.

"We'll fall!" Robert protested.

"That's the least of your worries. Go!"

Karina went first and Robert followed. He climbed in feetfirst, letting his legs dangle down into the shaft as Ms. Lavinia hurried him along.

"Just drop," she insisted. "Let yourself fall."

Instead, he reached out to plant both hands against the sides of the shaft, thinking he would lower himself inch by inch. But then gravity took over and he fell anyway.

The walls of the shaft blurred past him. Robert braced himself for the landing, waiting for the pain of impact to blast through his feet, shattering his ankles and knees.

Instead, the walls vanished into darkness and he seemed to decelerate—as if an invisible parachute had magically slowed his descent. Robert's body pitched forward and he put out his hands, trying to keep himself from landing headfirst.

He collapsed in a tumble on a cold, tiled floor. He rolled onto his back and realized he had landed in some kind of bathroom. Karina was standing beside a row of sinks, next to a paper towel dispenser.

"You okay?" she asked.

"Where are we?"

"Watch the gate," she said, pointing up to the ceiling.

Robert scrambled out of the way just in time. Glenn dropped out of the ceiling, collapsing in the same spot where Robert had landed moments earlier.

"Are we out? Is this Tillinghast? Or Lovecraft?" Glenn leapt to his feet and paced around the bathroom, searching for clues.

"It's Lovecraft," Karina said.

"I don't think so," Glenn said. "I've seen all the bathrooms at Lovecraft and I've never seen this one."

Something was weird about it, Robert agreed. It felt like a place where he didn't belong. There were no urinals—only stalls with doors. And the tiles were all pink and white. Mounted on the wall was a small box with a coin slot; it was some kind of vending machine.

"You guys are hilarious," Karina said. "You really don't know where you are?"

Suddenly the door to the bathroom opened and in walked Tracy Adams, a twelve-year-old girl from their Science class. She saw the boys and froze. It wasn't until this moment that Robert realized where they had landed: in a *girls'* bathroom.

And then he and Glenn were back on their feet and running again.

CHAPTER

SEVEN

That night, Glenn went over Robert's house for dinner. Glenn went over most nights, and Mrs. Arthur never complained. She said she liked having an extra person to help with the cleanup. If the boys finished their chores and homework early, they were allowed to watch TV or play video games together.

"Take more ravioli," she told Glenn, passing him the platter. "Someone needs to finish it."

"Mrs. Arthur, I'm stuffed," he said.

"You're sure? More salad?"

Glenn patted his stomach. "I can't. I'll explode."

She pushed herself away from the table and stood up. "You're both on kitchen duty tonight. I need to run

to the supermarket. I'm on the refreshments commit-
tee for the Halloween dance. Speaking of which, did
you buy your tickets yet?"

Robert and Glenn exchanged skeptical glances.

"You're not going?" Mrs. Arthur asked.

"Dances are lame," Robert said.

"Oh, come on," Mrs. Arthur said. "There must be
some pretty girl you'd like to invite. Maybe that Karina
you're always talking about?"

Robert blushed. "I don't think Karina can dance."

"All girls can dance," she said.

"It's hard to explain."

"Don't explain," Mrs. Arthur said, as she put on her
coat. "Just buy the tickets. I've already agreed to chap-
erone, so I want you boys to be there."

As soon as her car left the driveway, Pip and Squeak
came tumbling down the stairs. They leapt upon the
kitchen table, dove into the salad bowl, and began
chewing their way through a mound of greens and
sliced tomatoes.

"Careful," Robert told them. "Don't track salad

dressing all over the tablecloth."

Pip and Squeak had been living in a shoe box under Robert's bed for the past few weeks, but he had yet to tell his mother about them. She was terrified of regular household mice, so he could only imagine what she would make of a two-headed rat. He was forced to feed Pip and Squeak really late, after she went to bed, or on

those rare occasions when she left the house after dark.

While Glenn cleared the plates, Robert used a garden hose to fill the sink with water. A while back, the kitchen faucet had broken, so Mrs. Arthur had snaked a garden hose through the window. It was meant to be a temporary solution until she could scrape together enough money to hire a plumber, but they had been living with it for nearly a year.

"So what are we going to do?" Glenn asked.

He didn't need to elaborate. Robert knew he was talking about the Price sisters. The boys had spoken of nothing else since escaping Tillinghast Mansion earlier in the day.

"Watch our backs," Robert said. "Now that they're angry, I'm sure they'll come after us."

"Do you think they're demons? Like Professor Goyle?"

"They could be worse. There's two of them."

Just one month earlier, they discovered that their Science teacher, Professor Goyle, was in fact a giant winged demon named Azaroth. But Karina explained

65

that Tillinghast was summoning all kinds of monsters—giant insects, oozing slimes, savage beasts, and creatures beyond imagination. There was no telling what the Price sisters truly were—except strong, mean, and very dangerous.

"Maybe I should sleep over tonight," Glenn said. "Maybe I'm safer here."

There was a sudden loud knock at the front door.

The boys froze.

"Or maybe not," Robert said.

He dried his hands on a dish towel and then went out to the living room. He pulled back the curtains and peered outside.

"Who is it?" Glenn asked.

Robert opened the front door. Ms. Lavinia was standing on the porch, cradling a paper shopping bag.

"May I come in?" she asked.

"My mother's going to be back soon."

"I can't stay long."

Ms. Lavinia settled into the sofa. Robert and Glenn remained standing; they were too nervous to sit.

"You gentlemen did a very foolish thing today," she said.

"I know—" Robert began.

"Don't interrupt, Mr. Arthur. I want you to see what happens to humans who cross over to Tillinghast." She reached inside her bag, producing a ceramic container about the size of a one-gallon paint can. She unscrewed the lid and allowed the boys to peer inside. "This is where Crawford Tillinghast will keep your soul. Trapped for eternity on a shelf in his laboratory. While your body becomes a 'vessel' for one of his unholy minions. Do you gentlemen wish to spend the next thousand years living in a one-gallon ceramic jar?"

"No," Robert admitted. Glenn shook his head.

"Then I forbid you from crossing over ever again," Ms. Lavinia said. "It's simply too dangerous. If I hadn't been there . . ."

"Why *were* you there?" Robert said.

"I clean the house. I serve the food. I brew that hideous larval tea. My brother keeps me enslaved. If I refuse these tasks, he'll turn me over to his monsters."

"Your brother?" Robert and Glenn asked in unison.

"Yes, Crawford Tillinghast," Ms. Lavinia explained. "He's my twin."

CHAPTER

EIGHT

Ms. Lavinia explained that she was born Claudine Tillinghast at 10:25 a.m. on April 12, 1945. Her twin brother, Crawford, had been born just seven minutes earlier.

The children grew up in Tillinghast Mansion. For years, they were the best of friends. "It was a wonderful house back in the old days," she explained. "Warm, cheerful, full of light. My brother and I spent our days reading books and playing hide-and-seek. But everything changed after Crawford left for college and discovered his 'research.'"

As a young man studying physics, he pioneered a unique theory of alternate dimensions. Crawford believed there were worlds within our world—"invisible lands," he called them, occupied by ancient and powerful beasts. His classmates called him crazy. Even his professors mocked his wild ideas. Eventually Crawford became so disgusted, he dropped out of college.

Claudine was the only person who never lost faith in him. When Crawford returned to the family home, he used all his money to build a laboratory in its basement. "And I became his lab assistant," Ms. Lavinia explained, "because I was the only person who believed in him."

For years, they worked together in the laboratory, searching for invisible lands without success. The days were long. They rose at dawn and worked for twelve hours or more. Crawford constructed dozens of outrageous machines and Claudine worked alongside him, testing the devices and taking detailed notes. There were no vacations, no holidays, no time for anything resembling fun. Crawford only had time for research. He was obsessed.

"And then one morning something incredible happened," Ms. Lavinia continued. "Crawford sent me to the beach to collect some tidal pool specimens. Sea stars, anemones, barnacles—we were always running experiments on something. But that morning, there was another man on the beach. The handsomest man I'd ever met. You'll have to forgive the cliché, but it was love at first sight."

Soon Claudine was spending all her time with Warren Lavinia, a marine biologist who worked at the Dunwich Marine Museum and Lighthouse. They spent many wonderful hours together in a tall tower overlooking the rocky coast— such a sunny and cheerful place compared to Tillinghast's damp, dank basement laboratory.

When Crawford learned that his sister was marrying Warren—and leaving the lab—he was furious. He refused to attend her wedding, and he replaced Claudine with a team of scientists and their families.

"He called my marriage a betrayal. He said his work was far more important than any silly romance. I tried to make amends, but he never forgave me."

Then came the infamous fire, in which Crawford Tillinghast and seventeen other people lost their lives— or so she thought. "For thirty years I was happily married while Crawford was trapped in the alternaverse. But now that the gates are open, my brother is having his revenge. He keeps me enslaved. I clean his rooms, I prepare his meals, I serve his disgusting beasts like they're royalty. At night I sleep on a cold stone floor." She paused to check her wristwatch. "And if I leave Tillinghast or the school for more than an hour, he will send his monsters after my husband and kill him."

"That's not fair," Robert said.

"Can we stop him?" Glenn asked.

"I honestly don't think it's possible," said Ms. Lavinia. "With the gates open, he can access our world at will. He can capture students one by one and replace them with monsters. He's amassing an army like nothing the human world has ever seen. Even with all our weapons and computers, I don't think we're any match for it. Our best hope is to slow him down. To buy more time. I'm here tonight to ask for your help."

"Of course we'll help," Robert said.

"Totally," Glenn said. "We don't want to be stuck in jars for the rest of our lives. We'll do anything."

"Excellent," Ms. Lavinia said. "We need Robert to run for president of student council. And he needs to win. The election is Friday, so you'll have to work quickly."

At precisely that moment, Pip and Squeak came racing out of the kitchen, tracking salad dressing all over the linoleum floor. Robert grabbed a roll of paper towels and ran after them, wiping up their tracks. Once he had finished, the rats hopped onto the sofa and nuzzled their heads into Ms. Lavinia's belly. Robert expected her to be horrified, but instead she just scratched his pets behind their necks, like she was greeting baby kittens.

"You're such a cutie-pie," she whispered.

"Can we go back to what you said earlier?" Robert asked. "About student council?"

Ms. Lavinia nodded. "If Sarah wins this election, she will control the student body. And if she controls the student body, then it's only a matter of time before she *literally* controls the students' bodies. Do you understand?"

"But why me?" Robert asked. "Can't we help Howard Mergler win instead?"

Ms. Lavinia shook her head. "I have seen student councils come and go for thirty years. Mr. Mergler has good ideas and honest intentions. But he has no chance of beating Sarah Price."

"Then how about Glenn?"

"I'm afraid Mr. Torkells is ineligible. Too many disciplinary infractions." This was a polite way of saying that Glenn had a history of getting into trouble. At their previous school, he held the record for most detentions in a single year.

"I wish I could help," Robert said, "but I have no idea how to run for president."

"It's very simple," Ms. Lavinia said. "Tomorrow morning, you go see Mr. Loomis. He's the faculty advisor for student council. You ask him to put your name on the ballot, and I'll take care of the rest."

"But I can't win," Robert insisted. "I'm not a leader."

Ms. Lavinia shrugged. "Well, I'm afraid you need to become one."

CHAPTER

NINE

The next morning, before classes started, Robert went to see Mr. Loomis.

A lot of kids made fun of Mr. Loomis. He had a reputation for being a pushover. If you ever needed an extension for a book report because of a "sick grandmother," Mr. Loomis was the man to ask. And he was universally mocked for wearing pastel-colored sweater vests—pale yellow on Mondays, robin's-egg blue on Tuesdays, girly pink on Wednesdays, and so on, always in the same order, week after week.

So Robert never admitted to anyone, not even to Glenn, that Mr. Loomis was his favorite teacher at Lovecraft Middle School. He taught language arts,

Robert's favorite subject, and he was always writing encouraging notes at the bottom of Robert's assignments: *You have good ideas*, the most recent one said. *You should share more in class!*

When Robert arrived, Mr. Loomis was sitting at his desk, eating a bran muffin and reading the local newspaper, the *Dunwich Chronicle*. "Hey, Robert, listen to this," he said. "A woman was walking on the docks last week? Down by the water? And she swears she saw a leprechaun swimming out of the ocean. 'She described the creature as a tiny man, three inches tall.'" Mr. Loomis shook his head. "People are crazy."

"I want to run for president," Robert said.

"Right, exactly!" Mr. Loomis said. "'I want to be a movie star!' 'There are leprechauns on our beaches!' Where do people get this stuff?"

"No, I'm serious," Robert insisted. "I want to lead the student council."

Mr. Loomis closed his newspaper. "The election is Friday. Two days from now. Sarah Price has been campaigning for weeks."

"I can win," Robert said.

Mr. Loomis shook his head. "Not in two days, you can't. She's got momentum. It's too late. Why don't you try out for Handwriting Club? They always need fresh faces."

"I want to be president," Robert said.

"Why?"

Robert realized he lacked a convincing answer to this question. *Because Ms. Lavinia told me to? Because the Price sisters are monsters in disguise? Because they're planning to capture the soul of every student attending Lovecraft Middle School?*

"Look, Robert, I'm going to be frank," Mr. Loomis said. "I know you were redistricted. I know all your old classmates are at Franklin Middle School and you got stuck here. You don't know anyone and that stinks. Am I right?"

"Yes."

"So let me ask you a tough question. And I'm sorry if this sounds mean. But who do you think is going to vote for you?"

"I don't know," Robert admitted. He knew Mr. Loomis was right. Robert's only friends at Lovecraft were a bully, a ghost, and a two-headed rat—and only one of those friends could actually pull a voting lever. "I guess I just want to try. I don't care if I lose. Our school deserves better than Sarah Price. Deep down inside, I think she's a . . . monster."

Mr. Loomis shook his head. "I won't tolerate name-calling in this election. You can disagree with her policies, but I don't want to hear any personal attacks. You keep it clean. Do you understand?"

"Are you saying you'll do it?" Robert asked. "You'll put me on the ballot?"

Mr. Loomis's reply was lost under the sudden wail of a blaring siren. Lovecraft Middle School was equipped with a state-of-the-art fire safety system. Whenever an alarm was triggered, the siren could be heard in every corner of the school, and all doors automatically unlocked, so that no student would be trapped in the blaze. Robert and Mr. Loomis were hurrying to the door when the alarm stopped short and

Principal Slater's voice came over the PA system. "Please excuse that test of our emergency alert system," she said. "I repeat, the alarm has been canceled."

Mr. Loomis pinched the bridge of his nose, as if he was fending off a sudden headache. "Every time that stupid alarm goes off, I feel like I'm losing my mind," he complained. "What were we talking about?"

"The ballot," Robert said. "Will you put me on?"

"If you insist on being part of the election, yes," Mr. Loomis said. "But you'd better start preparing for the presidential debate on Friday morning. I'm asking tough questions and the whole school will be watching. You don't want to embarrass yourself."

Mr. Loomis explained that Robert would need to sign a written application and then went to the main office to retrieve it. Robert sat at a desk and waited for him to return. His ears were still ringing from the alarm, so he didn't hear soft footsteps sneaking into the classroom; he didn't see Sarah and Sylvia until they were nearly on top of him.

"This is so disappointing," Sarah said. "Master is

very upset."

"And now you're making things worse," Sylvia said.
"You think you can defeat my sister?"

Sarah laughed. "He's just a child. Look at that baby

face! No one will vote for him."

Robert rose from the desk but he was unable to back away. There was something hypnotic about their gaze; his feet felt anchored to the floor. He tried to look brave.

"We know you're scared," Sarah said, and her long purple tongue flicked out of her lips, dripping gooey saliva. Her pupils narrowed to thin vertical slits. "We can smell your fear."

Sylvia reached for Robert's wrist. Her fingers were cool and dry, like the texture of a leather shoe. "And we know about your nightmares. Master is keeping his eyes on you. You're wise to be afraid."

They took turns whispering to him:

"Tell Loomis you made a mistake."

"Tell him you changed your mind."

"You're just a child."

"You're too weak to fight us."

And Robert knew they were right—he *was* too weak. He was too scared even to make eye contact. How was he going to debate them in front of the entire school?

"Allrighty, I'm back!" Mr. Loomis announced, entering the classroom with paperwork in hand. "Oh, hello, girls! Did Robert share his big news?"

In an instant, Sarah retracted her tongue and her pupils popped back to normal. "It's wonderful!"

"We're so excited!" Sylvia gushed. "Democracy flourishes with competition!"

Mr. Loomis placed the application in front of Robert, handed him a pen, and showed him where to sign. "Last chance to back out," he warned. "Are you sure you *really* want to do this?"

"No," Robert said, but he went ahead and put his signature on the document anyway. He felt like he was signing his life away.

CHAPTER

TEN

At lunchtime, Ms. Lavinia invited Robert, Glenn, and Karina to her office in the back of the library, where they met with the shades drawn and the doors locked. "If my brother learns I'm helping you, he'll rip my head off," she said. "And that's not what your language arts teachers call hyperbole."

They had gathered to make campaign posters. Ms. Lavinia had prepared a large worktable and supplies—different colors of paper, magic markers, glue sticks, scissors. "We're going to start by identifying your message. The thing that makes you different from the other candidates. Sarah Price is pretty and popular. Howard Mergler is smart with big ideas. Robert Arthur needs to give students a third choice." She leaned over a poster with a marker, scrawled a single word, and then held it up for them to read: STRENGTH.

"I don't get it," Robert said.

"This is your message," Ms. Lavinia explained. "You're strong."

Glenn laughed. "Have you seen his biceps? They're like chicken wings! My grandmother has more meat on her bones!"

Robert cringed at the jokes but knew they were true. Yesterday's incident in the swimming pool was only the most recent demonstration of his weakness. In gym class, whenever Coach Glandis led the students through their daily dozen push-ups, Robert could never keep pace. He was always far behind the other boys.

"Glenn's right," he admitted. "I don't think I should brag about my muscles."

"You're confusing muscles with strength," Ms. Lavinia said. "They're two different things. Muscle is animal tissue that contracts to produce force or motion. Strength is a character trait. It's resolution, determination, making difficult choices . . ."

Robert had already stopped listening. Nothing Ms. Lavinia said would change the fact that he weighed ninety pounds and still needed help opening jars of spaghetti sauce. In the world of seventh-graders, this made him a grade-A weakling.

Together they formed an assembly line. Ms. Lavinia began each poster by writing a slogan in large block letters. Karina offered color suggestions, and Robert and Glenn inked the letters with different shades of magic marker. Each time a poster was finished, Pip and Squeak would emerge from a tray of glitter glue and walk its perimeter, framing it with sparkles. The work was slow and tedious, and after just ten posters, Glenn complained that his fingers were cramping.

"If you think you're cramped now, try spending the rest of your life in a one-gallon jar," Ms. Lavinia said, slapping another piece of paper in front of him. "Keep coloring."

They worked through lunch, and after school Robert and Karina returned to make more. Each poster offered a different message about Robert's extraordinary strength. ROBERT ARTHUR FIGHTS FOR YOU. ROBERT ARTHUR WILL NOT BACK DOWN. ROBERT ARTHUR WILL NOT GIVE UP. Robert felt like the posters were describing someone other than himself—a fictional Super-Robert who was bigger and braver than his real-life counterpart.

At the end of the afternoon, Robert and Karina walked to the nearest exit.

Since there were no other students around, he allowed Pip and Squeak to walk freely behind them. The rats loved any opportunity to get out of the backpack.

"So what do you do at night?" he asked Karina. "After everyone leaves?"

"I spend a lot of time hiding from janitors," she said. "Once they leave, I can listen to music in the band room. Or I'll read in the library. The nurse's office has a nice cot for lying down." It sounded awfully lonely to Robert. He didn't say anything, but Karina spoke as if she'd read his mind. "The nights aren't bad, but the weekends are terrible. Saturdays and Sundays drag on forever."

"Maybe you can come to my house sometime," he suggested.

"I wish I could," she said, "but it doesn't work that way."

She didn't elaborate and Robert didn't press for details. He knew she was confined to the grounds of Lovecraft Middle School but didn't understand why. Whenever he asked Karina about her life as a ghost, she always changed the subject, as if she preferred to be seen as a living, breathing, flesh-and-blood girl.

"Let me ask you something," Karina said. "What are you wearing tomorrow?"

"I don't know," Robert said. "Clothes?"

"You can't wear just anything. You're running for office now. You need to dress like a leader."

"What, like a suit?"

"Wear your red shirt with the little squares. And tuck it in, okay?"

Robert saluted her. "Aye, aye, Captain."

She scowled and swatted his arm. Her fingers

passed right through him, raising goose bumps on his flesh, and he fought the urge to shiver. "You can win this thing," she said. "I know you don't think so, but I do. I believe in you."

An awkward moment passed. Robert had recently decided that ghost kids were different from regular kids. Karina talked more than any human friend he'd ever had. She offered advice on what clothes he should wear and often she surprised him by saying the nicest things, like "I believe in you." The kids at his old school would never say things like "I believe in you." Sometimes Robert didn't know how to answer her.

"Well, good night," he finally said. "Watch out for janitors."

"You, too."

"Me, too?"

"*Good night* to you, too," Karina said, flustered, already retreating into the shadowy hallways of the school. "See you tomorrow."

CHAPTER

ELEVEN

Robert was determined to get stronger, so he devoted the entire evening to exercise. He practiced all the calisthenics he'd learned in gym class: sit-ups, jumping jacks, leg lifts, and lunges. And once an hour, he lay down on the floor of his bedroom and forced himself to do push-ups. At eight o'clock, he did fifteen in a row. At nine o'clock, he did half as many. By ten o'clock, he barely squeezed out three and a quarter.

Then he stumbled into the bathroom, unbuttoned his shirt, and examined himself in the mirror, studying his physique for signs of change. His biceps looked the same—but the muscles in his chest seemed . . . well, if not bigger, then definitely *swollen*. Was it his imagination? Robert turned left and right, studying his body from different angles. It was hard to tell.

Mrs. Arthur walked past the door. "What are you doing?"

Robert buttoned his shirt. "Nothing."

She squeezed behind him, studying their reflections in the bathroom mirror. "I hope you're not worried about your looks. You're going to make a very handsome president."

Mrs. Arthur had been thrilled to learn that Robert was running for student council. She seemed to believe that he had an excellent chance of winning, that everyone in Lovecraft Middle School loved Robert as much as she did.

There were times, Robert thought, when his mother simply didn't have a clue.

After tucking Pip and Squeak into their shoe box, Robert got into bed and fell asleep immediately; all the exercise had made him very tired. That night, he had another dream, and for once it wasn't a nightmare. He was back at Lovecraft Middle School with Karina

Ortiz, and she was telling him to wear the red shirt with the little squares, and then she playfully swatted his shoulder. Only this time, her fingers didn't pass through his skin. This time, her hand was warm and solid and real. *She* was real.

Robert looked into her eyes, astonished.

"I know," she said, grinning. "Isn't it crazy?"

He woke up shivering. His alarm clock read 3:13. He pulled his blankets up to his shoulders and turned over in bed, trying to return to the dream. He willed himself to fall asleep, but he was too cold to concentrate. He was *freezing*.

He sat up in bed.

His window was open.

That was weird. Robert often propped his window open during the summer, but never after Labor Day. It was now the end of October, when the night temperature could dip as low as thirty degrees.

Maybe his mother had opened it?

A frigid wind whipped through the room, fluttering the posters taped over the bed, threatening to rip their corners from the walls.

He wished there was some way to close the window without leaving the warmth of the blankets. He lay there for a moment, mustering the willpower to stand. And in that moment his toes nudged something smooth and cool and dry, something with the texture of a leather shoe. Robert was always falling asleep with books in his bed. Maybe tonight he had fallen asleep with a shoe?

But then the "shoe" moved, sliding over and under his ankles, binding his feet together. Robert lifted the blanket and saw two glowing yellow eyes; their pupils were thin vertical slits. He tried yanking his legs out of bed but he was already too late; the snake coiled around his knees, thighs, and hips, immobilizing him from the waist down. The more Robert struggled to get free, the easier it was for the snake to encircle the rest of him, pinning his arms to his sides and anchoring his torso to the mattress. Every time Robert exhaled, the snake coiled itself tighter, slowing the circulation of his bloodstream. His hands and feet were already tingling. Finally Robert closed his eyes and willed himself to wake up.

Because it *had* to be a dream. It simply had to be. Boa constrictors couldn't open windows. Massachusetts didn't even *have* boa constrictors. This was just like the dream where Principal Slater turned into a frog monster. Any moment now, Robert's mother would open the door and turn on the light and the snake would disappear . . .

"Give up, Robert."

He opened his eyes.

"Quit now and we'll go easy on you."

The snake's mouth hadn't opened but Robert could hear it speaking—or, rather, he could hear Sarah and Sylvia speaking, as plainly as if they were standing right beside him. Robert would have said "Okay" if he'd been capable of saying anything—but he lacked the strength to even nod his head. The edges of his vision were going dark. The room was fading. He felt like he was back underwater, stuck at the bottom of the swimming pool with no gate in sight.

Then Pip and Squeak stumbled out from under the bed, drawn by the unfamiliar voices. They saw the snake and immediately sprang into attack mode, leaping onto Robert's nightstand and toppling his lamp. It fell to the ground with a crash. The boa hissed. Pip and Squeak leaned back on their haunches, baring their teeth.

"Robert?" Mrs. Arthur called from her bedroom. "What's that noise?"

"Don't come in," Robert tried to shout, only no sounds could leave his mouth, not anymore.

The hallway light came on, filling the gap under Robert's bedroom door with a pale yellow glow. The boa gave him one last warning—a squeeze that nearly made his heart pop like a balloon—before uncoiling itself and darting toward the open window. Mrs. Arthur's frantic footsteps were already coming down the hallway. As the last of the snake disappeared through the window, Pip and Squeak hurried under the bed just as the door opened, flooding the room with light.

His nightstand lamp lay in broken pieces on the floor.

"What happened?" Mrs. Arthur asked.

Robert couldn't speak. He was still catching his breath.

"And why is your window open? It's freezing in here!"

She walked over to the window and slammed it shut.

"I'm sorry," he said. "I was just having another nightmare. I reached for my light and I guess I knocked it over."

"See, that's the thing I hate about Halloween," Mrs. Arthur said. "They put all these violent movies on television and then kids can't sleep at night. We're cutting back on screen time, Robert, do you understand me?"

"All right," he said.

"And you need to be more careful. Lamps cost money!"

After his mother had left the room and closed the

door, Robert got out of bed and walked over to his window. Under the light of a full moon, his backyard was bathed in a soft pale glow. He could see the boa slithering across the grass, crossing toward a hedge at the rear of the lawn.

Standing behind the hedge, waiting for the snake, were two silhouettes of human figures—two identical silhouettes. Robert couldn't see their faces, yet he knew exactly who they were.

CHAPTER

TWELVE

The next morning, Robert went to school early and walked the hallways with a stack of posters and a roll of masking tape, hanging advertisements every ten feet or so. Sometimes he heard kids reading the posters and giggling.

"Who the heck is Robert Arthur?"

"Beats me."

"Never heard of him."

Robert knew these were perfect opportunities to introduce himself. A real leader would turn around and shake hands and tell the kids exactly why they should vote for him. But Robert was afraid they would laugh or make fun of him or worse. The poster presented him as a valiant warrior, but after last night he felt more frightened and inadequate than ever.

He was taping a poster in the boys' bathroom when he was startled by a loud clatter of metal. He turned to see Howard Mergler struggling to push open the door. Howard had dropped one of his forearm crutches and was trying to retrieve it. The orthotic braces on his legs made it impossible to bend his knees. He looked like he was about to topple over.

"Here," Robert said, grabbing the crutch for him.

"Thanks," Howard said. "You would not believe how often that happens."

Robert returned to taping his poster.

"So it's true?" Howard asked. "You're running for president?"

"It's true. Nothing personal."

"Let me give you some free advice," Howard said. "Don't say you're going to give students better computer equipment. Or more nutritious school lunches."

"Why not?"

"Because I'm saying that, and no one listens!"

Robert laughed. "It's too bad. Those are good ideas."

"They're great ideas. But who can compete with Cupcake Friday? That's what Sarah Price is promising. Free cupcakes in the lobby every Friday. Never mind who makes them, or who pays for them." Howard sighed. "People love her and they're going to vote for her. We don't have a chance."

At lunch, Robert went to the library and told Ms. Lavinia about the giant snake. "It told me to drop out, and I think I should."

Ms. Lavinia scoffed. "Now why would you listen to a snake?" She was pushing her wooden cart through a corridor lined with books and Robert hustled to keep up.

"Well, for starters, this snake was in my bed. And it was a hundred feet long. It was very persuasive."

She absently plucked a book from a shelf and added it to the cart. "You can't quit now. We're running a great campaign. You just need to stick with it."

"The election's tomorrow. All I've done is hang

posters!"

"That's phase one of the plan. My husband will help with phase two."

"Your husband?"

"Warren Lavinia. You can find him in the old lighthouse down by the waterfront." She pulled a pink envelope from her pocket and handed it to Robert. "Give him these instructions and he'll take care of the rest."

"Can you come with me?"

"I wish I could. My brother forbids it. But you can take Glenn." She thought for a moment. "And go as early as you can. You boys don't want to be at the waterfront after dark."

CHAPTER

THIRTEEN

Long ago, Dunwich was home to a thriving seaport, full of fishermen, lobstermen, and even whalers. All those industries eventually moved away but the old docks remained, a twisting, splintered maze of wooden planks. By the time Robert and Glenn arrived at the waterfront, the sun was already setting. Seagulls circled the sky, screeching and squalling. There were no other people around so Robert unzipped his backpack and allowed Pip and Squeak to walk behind them.

"This place stinks," Glenn said.

"Like larval tea," Robert agreed.

The lighthouse was a skinny five-story tower that reminded Robert of the Rapunzel story. A weathered

sign was nailed to the front of the door: PULL ROPE
FOR SERVICE.

He looked up. Above his head—and nearly out of
reach—was the frayed end of a tattered cord. It extended fifty feet straight up, all the way to the top of the
lighthouse.

Robert tugged on the rope and listened.

"Did you hear anything?" he asked.

"Try it again," Glenn said.

This time, they both listened carefully. It was hard
to hear anything over the sounds of the waves crashing
against the rocky shores.

"There!" Glenn said, pointing.

Robert looked up. There was a small balcony ringing the top of the lighthouse. A man wearing a scuba
mask leaned over its railing.

"Not interested!" he shouted.

Robert looked to Glenn. "Not interested?"

"He thinks we're selling something. Girl Scout
cookies, I don't know."

Robert cupped his hands around his mouth and

shouted, "Your wife sent us!" but it was too late—
Warren had already left the balcony. Between the waves
and the screeching seagulls, he hadn't heard a thing.

They waited outside another few minutes, until it
was clear that Warren wasn't returning to the balcony
or coming downstairs to open the door.

"Now what?" Glenn asked.

"I don't know," Robert said.

A seagull landed beside them and stamped its feet
impatiently. Robert wished he could ask the bird to deliver a message. Then Pip and Squeak came charging
over, playfully baring their fangs and chasing the bird
away.

"I've got it," he said.

He removed the pink envelope from his backpack
and knelt beside Pip and Squeak. "I need you guys to
make a delivery."

His pets never failed to impress him with their in-
telligence. They seemed capable of understanding virtually everything Robert said. He believed this was
because they had twice the brains of an ordinary rat.

Pip took the note in his mouth, and Robert raised the rats over his head, holding them steady until they had grasped the rope with their claws.

"That's it," he said. "All the way up to the top. Take your time and be careful. Give the note to the man."

Robert held the rope taut and the rats advanced slowly but steadily, stopping only when a strong wind blew off the ocean and strummed the rope like a guitar string. After another minute or so, the rats reached the summit and disappeared over the railing.

Robert was still looking up at the sky, waiting for Warren to return, when he noticed a tiny object hurtling toward him. Robert leapt aside and a heavy silver key landed in the gravel at his feet. It fit perfectly into the lock of the front door.

"Mission accomplished," Glenn said.

It was Robert's first time inside a lighthouse, and he was surprised to see that it consisted almost entirely of a single spiral staircase. It seemed to stretch toward the sky into infinity.

"No wonder he doesn't want to come down,"

Glenn said.

Robert grabbed the handrail and began to climb. Every fifteen steps or so, they passed a small window cut into the side of the building; they could see the waterfront docks getting smaller and smaller. Halfway up, Robert felt winded, but since Glenn was having no trouble following along, he kept his complaints to himself.

At the top of the stairs, they emerged into a small round room with glass walls. It was a mess. Papers, charts, and maps were strewn across the floor; workbenches were cluttered with vials, test tubes, and other lab apparatus.

In the center of the room stood an elderly man dressed in a neoprene wet suit and swim fins. He looked like he had just emerged from the ocean—his hair was wet and water was still dripping down his body—but he was focusing all his attention on Pip and Squeak, offering them slices of fresh apple from his hand.

"Hello," Robert said. "I'm—"

"I know who you are, I read the note," Warren said,

dismissing introductions with a wave of his hand. "I'm conducting an experiment and I need your help." He directed the boys to a workbench containing three lemons, a wooden cutting board, and a serrated knife. "Cut these into quarters. Big fat chunks."

"But Ms. Lavinia wants—"

"Chop, chop, chop," Warren said. "Hurry, please."

Robert realized Warren wasn't going to listen, so he picked up the knife and set to work. Meanwhile, Warren carried over a small glass aquarium about the size of a shoe box. Pacing inside on a bed of blue gravel was a large hermit crab with a magnificent spiral-coiled shell. The hermit crab seemed exceptionally lively, marching in circles around its tank.

"I plucked this fellow straight from the ocean." Warren opened the lid of the aquarium, then tapped the crab's shell with the point of his pencil. "Do you see the exoskeleton? Do you hear the *tap-tap-tap*? Very hard, very brittle, right? That's calcium carbonate. A very convincing disguise. But look what even a mild acid can do."

Warren took a lemon wedge and squeezed it over the crab. Tiny plumes of smoke arose from the shell, as if it had somehow been ignited.

"What are you doing?" Glenn asked.

"Don't worry, the crab doesn't feel any pain," Warren assured him. He squeezed the lemon again, squirting more citric acid onto the shell. "He's not even a real crab."

More smoke billowed out. The once-brittle shell was dissolving into a mound of quivering, translucent gray goo. It looked like the world's most disgusting serving of Jell-O.

"You killed it?" Robert asked.

"I *exposed* it. Watch careful now, see the little arms and legs?"

Robert and Glenn peered into the tank. Within the mound of gray goo, they could just discern a tiny human figure, punching and kicking at the sides, like an insect escaping from its cocoon. The creature was no bigger than a thumb. Its body had the slimy green scales of a dragon. It had two long flippers for arms but walked on two legs, like a miniature person.

The most dramatic difference was its head. The creature had tiny eyes and nostrils, but its mouth was hidden by a dozen mini tentacles that hung from the bottom of its face like party streamers. As the creature emerged from the goo, slapping away the slime, Robert could hear it droning in a tinny high-pitched voice.

"What is it?" Glenn whispered.

"Cthulhu," Warren said, pronouncing the word *ka-THOO-loo*, and then he gestured to the ocean outside the windows. "The shore is full of them. Hundreds, maybe thousands." He lowered salad tongs into the tank and used them to pinch the cthulhu's waist. The creature hissed and yelled and frantically waved its flippers.

Warren carried it across the room to a larger aquarium. This one was filled with more cthulhus, at least three dozen of them, sitting and standing and pacing in circles, little convicts in a miniature prison. The sound of their tinny voices crescendoed as Warren raised the lid and deposited the newest arrival inside.

"Where are they coming from?" Glenn asked.

"Your school. The gates. Every day, dozens of these tiny creatures come creeping out." Warren walked his fingers across a tabletop, mimicking the footsteps of a cthulu. "They're beneath our shoes, they're barely visible, we never notice them. But soon, believe me, we will notice. Soon, they'll grow too big to ignore."

"We're trying to help," Robert explained. "Ms. Lavinia wants me to run for class president. The election is Friday—"

Warren nodded. "I read my wife's note. But I think she's mistaken. You boys are too young for this war. You wouldn't last five minutes in the alternaverse. Tillinghast's mansion has creatures more horrific than anything you can imagine. Spiders, demons, eyeslime . . ."

"We know," Glenn interrupted.

Warren shook his head. "You can't know until you've been there."

"Right," Glenn said, "we've *been there*."

Warren peered at the boys over the top of his glasses. "Wait a second. Are you saying you've crossed over? And made it back alive?"

Robert nodded. "A few times."

"Well, why didn't Claudine mention that in her letter?" He looked at them with a newfound respect. "You two boys are stronger than you look! This is good, very good!" He stood up and paced around the room, tapping his fingertip to his chin. "The trick, I think, is demonstrating your strength to your classmates—but how? Will you have an opportunity to address the school?"

"The candidate debate is tomorrow morning," Glenn said. "It's a mandatory assembly. All the students and teachers will be there."

"Perfect." Warren removed a stack of yellow legal pads from his shelf, carried them over to his workbench, and copied a passage onto an index card. "Now I want you to follow these instructions carefully. Wait until your classmates are assembled. And then recite this incantation three times."

Robert read the card. "*K'yaloh f'ah*—"

"No, no, stop," Warren interrupted. "I don't need my lab destroyed, thank you very much. Save it for tomorrow."

"Destroyed?" Robert asked. "What's going to happen?"

"Nothing you can't handle. Just remember, its beak is worse than its bite."

"You mean, its *bark* is worse than its bite?"

"That, too." Warren gave Pip and Squeak one last scratch behind the ears. "Now run along before it gets dark. And give my wife a message for me. Tell her we'll be together soon, okay? Sooner than she thinks."

CHAPTER

FOURTEEN

The auditorium at Lovecraft Middle School seated five hundred at the orchestra level and another one hundred and fifty in the balcony. The room's most stunning feature was a large glass dome; it cast a warm, natural light across the stage. Under normal circumstances, it would have been a pleasant and relaxing space.

But for Robert the circumstances were anything but normal. He sat at a table in the center of the stage, sipping nervously from a glass of water, watching students and teachers file into their chairs. It was the start of first period, and the debate assembly would begin in a few moments.

Sarah Price sat on Robert's left. She smiled at the

audience and waved to some friends in the fourth row. "You should have joined us while you had the chance," she whispered to Robert, still smiling and waving. "You will pay for your betrayal. Your surrender will be especially painful."

Robert didn't answer. He knew that Sarah was telling the truth. He had heard enough things about Crawford Tillinghast to know that the man had a flair for cruel and unusual punishment.

Howard Mergler was seated on Robert's right. He had come to the debate armed with a solar calculator, five newly sharpened pencils, and several notebooks' worth of ideas and arguments, all of them meticulously tabbed and cross-referenced.

"Well, good luck to you," Howard said, clapping him on the shoulder. "May the best candidate win."

"Thanks," Robert said. "And same to you. It seems like you've really done your homework."

"Not that it matters," Howard shrugged. "You'll see. But I'll give it my best shot anyway."

Principal Slater and Ms. Lavinia had seats near the

front of the auditorium, and somehow Glenn scored a seat in the first row. The words ROBERT ARTHUR FOR STUDENT COUNCIL PRESIDENT were scrawled in black magic marker across the front of his T-shirt, and he was holding a large cardboard sign that read ROBERT FOR PREZ—HE'S AWESOME!

Mr. Loomis stood behind a tall podium decorated with the Lovecraft school crest. "Please take your seats, everyone," he said. "We'd like to get started."

Robert felt his stomach do a little flip. He'd never liked speaking in front of groups, and he'd never addressed a group as large as this one. As people settled into their chairs, he glimpsed Karina lingering at the back of the auditorium. She smiled and mouthed the words "Good luck."

"Welcome, students and faculty," Mr. Loomis began. "It is my great pleasure to introduce the candidates for student council president: Sarah Price—"

At the mere mention of Sarah's name, the audience burst into excited applause and a chant of "Sa-rah! Sa-rah!" echoed through the room. Mr. Loomis waved his

arms and called for quiet, to no avail. It wasn't until
Principal Slater stood up—and glared at everyone in
the auditorium—that students finally settled down.

"As I was saying," Mr. Loomis continued, "we have
Sarah Price, Howard Mergler, and Robert Arthur."

"Let's GO, Rob-ERT!" Glenn chanted, pounding
a cadence on the armrest of his chair. "Let's GO, Rob-
ERT!" But none of the other students joined in the
chant, and Glenn's voice trailed off.

"The first question goes to Howard Mergler," Mr.
Loomis began. "If you win the election, what will be
your first action as student council president?"

Howard offered a four-part answer involving health-
ier school lunches, faster computer equipment, longer
after-school hours for library patrons, and improved access for handicapped students. Robert liked all these ideas
but found his attention wandering as Howard spoke.
There was some polite applause when Howard finished,
mostly from the teachers in the audience.

"I'll pose the same question to Sarah Price," Mr.
Loomis said, and again the audience erupted with

applause at the mention of her name. "If you win the election, Sarah, what will be your first action as student council president?"

Sarah beamed at the crowd. "I'm going to give you the best, because Lovecraft students deserve the best! You're smart. You're bright. You're good-looking. Why should you settle for less? You deserve the best classes. The best teachers. The best schedules. The best dances. If you want the best, vote for the best. Vote Sarah Price. Thanks, guys, you're the best!"

Robert listened in disbelief. Sarah had answered the question without actually answering the question. She had simply complimented everyone in the audience. Yet again the applause was overwhelming. Students were on their feet chanting "Sa-rah! Sa-rah!" and Mr. Loomis spent five minutes shushing everyone.

"Same question to Robert Arthur," Mr. Loomis continued. "If you win the election, Robert, what will be your first action as student council president?"

The auditorium fell silent.

Robert stared out at the audience. Hundreds of

faces stared back. A few kids were already snickering. He paused to take a sip of water. He thought of his campaign slogans, of Ms. Lavinia's poster messages. "Um, I guess I'll protect you?"

The audience laughed, and Robert's face flushed. *Of course* they laughed. How was this scrawny ninety-pound kid going to protect anyone from anything?

Even Mr. Loomis was smiling. "Protect *me*?"

"I'll protect the school."

"You're allowed two minutes for your answer," Mr. Loomis told him. "Maybe you should elaborate."

But Robert didn't know what else to say. He couldn't deliver a fake answer like Sarah Price, he couldn't articulate a smart answer like Howard Mergler, and he certainly couldn't tell the truth. He had only one card left to play—so he removed it from his pocket and read the words Warren had written:

"*K'yaloh f'ah Zhenz'koh.*"

"Excuse me?" Mr. Loomis asked.

Robert leaned forward into his microphone. "*K'yaloh f'ah Zhenz'koh.*"

Sarah glared at him. "Don't you dare," she hissed.

Mr. Loomis furrowed his brow. "Robert, I can't make out what you're saying. Move back from the microphone and try it again."

"*K'yaloh f'ah Zhenz'koh.*"

Nothing happened. It didn't work. The students in the audience were cracking up. It was their first good look at Robert Arthur and he was spouting gibberish like an idiot.

Mr. Loomis left his podium and walked over to the table. "We must be having technical difficulties because I can't understand a word you're—"

He was interrupted by an ear-splitting screech. Robert's water glass shattered, spraying shards across the table. Students collapsed in their seats, crying out in pain, covering their ears.

Robert looked up to the empty balcony and there, hovering above the last row of seats, was a swirling black vortex. An enormous creature emerged from it, flying out over the auditorium. It was some kind of giant bird, swooping toward the stage.

Sarah ran screaming into the audience.

Howard fumbled for his crutches.

Robert froze.

This was Warren's brilliant idea? Summoning a giant bird to attack the entire school?

As the creature hurtled toward him, Robert realized it wasn't *entirely* a bird—it had the head of a monstrous woman. Like the harpies from ancient mythology. It flew with its giant talons extended, ready to pluck Robert off the ground. When he was close enough to see its eyes, he dove out of his chair, knocking Howard Mergler onto the floor and dragging him to safety beneath the table.

"What is that thing?" Howard shouted.

"I have no idea," Robert said.

Out in the audience, pandemonium ensued. The harpy was circling the theater in preparation for a second assault, beating its filthy wings and raining dusty feathers upon the assembly below. Robert looked for Glenn, for Karina, for Ms. Lavinia—anyone who could tell him what to do. But the faces were all a blur. He was on his own.

"Remain calm!" Mr. Loomis shouted into his microphone. "Please proceed to the nearest exit in a calm and orderly fashion!"

The winged beast heard Mr. Loomis and shrieked again, changing course and diving toward the teacher with its talons extended. Robert shouted at Mr. Loomis to get down, to get out of the way; the harpy's claws were aimed straight at his face.

It wasn't fair. Mr. Loomis had gone out of his way to be nice to Robert, to make sure he was doing well at Lovecraft. And now he was going to get hurt, all because Robert had summoned some stupid monster from Tillinghast.

He scrambled to his feet, reached behind the curtain, and grabbed one of the music stands used by the orchestra. It was four feet tall and surprisingly heavy, with all the heft of an aluminum baseball bat. He elbowed Mr. Loomis out of the way and then swung the music stand with all his might, striking the harpy in the side. The creature released another ear-splitting shriek

and soared skyward, toward the glass dome in the ceiling above the stage.

"What's happening?" Mr. Loomis asked.

"Move!" Robert shouted, taking his teacher by the arm and dragging him to the table where Howard was still hiding. "Get down! Quick! Cover your—"

Before he could say "ears," the harpy crashed through the ceiling, shattering the glass dome into thousands of deadly projectiles. Some were as thin as fingernails; others were as wide and sharp as the blades of a guillotine; all of them came raining down on Robert and Mr. Loomis. He pushed his teacher underneath the table and squeezed in beside him, just as the first shards hit the stage. Robert closed his eyes and covered his face with his hands. The noise was cacophonous and seemed to last forever, like a thunderstorm that wouldn't end, a thousand broken windows shattering all around them.

And then, silence.

Robert peeled his hands away from his face. Except for their tiny sanctuary beneath the table, the stage was covered with mounds of shattered glass, piled high like sands on a beach.

Tiny flecks of glass were embedded in the backs of Robert's hands, but otherwise he was unharmed.

So were Howard and Mr. Loomis. Robert grabbed Howard's forearm crutches and helped the boy to his feet.

"Is it gone?" Howard asked.

Robert glanced up at the ceiling and saw a gaping hole where the dome had been. "I think so."

And somewhere in these moments, he realized he was still being watched. The auditorium was still full of people. All of his classmates and teachers had witnessed the spectacle in astonished disbelief. And there was Ms. Lavinia sitting among them, hands folded in her lap and looking rather pleased with phase two of her plan.

CHAPTER
FIFTEEN

The human imagination is strange and unpredictable. In the hours following the student council debate, everyone was discussing how Robert Arthur saved Mr. Loomis from a huge hawk. Or a giant falcon. Or a crazed owl. Hundreds of people had witnessed the attack, but no two people could agree on exactly what they had seen. They could only agree that it was amazing and awesome and spectacular.

Eddie Milano had snapped some pictures with his cell phone but they were too blurry to settle any arguments. The best one showed Robert standing between Mr. Loomis and the creature, gripping the music stand like a baseball bat, determined and ready to strike.

Glenn came running up to Robert after second period. "Check this out!" He'd copied the photograph onto a flyer and transformed it into a campaign poster. VOTE ROBERT ARTHUR, the headline read. HE FIGHTS FOR YOU! "I made two hundred copies of these and I'm already wiped out. People are hanging them in their lockers. You've gone viral, man! You're a superstar!"

Teachers praised his quick thinking and bravery. Kids he'd never met were high-fiving him in the hallways. Someone left a note in his locker, requesting an interview for the school newspaper. And Mr. Loomis ended fourth-period English class by expressing his gratitude.

"Fear plays tricks on the mind," he explained to the class. "When I saw that bird swooping toward me, I didn't see a bird. I saw an honest-to-goodness monster. With wild eyes and dripping fangs. I was so scared, I couldn't move!" He paused to chuckle at his own foolishness. "Anyhow, I'm glad that cooler heads prevailed. Thank you, Robert."

The class applauded and the lunch bell rang and

then it was time for seventh-graders to go to the cafeteria and choose their student council representatives. The school had borrowed real voting booths from the township; they looked like tall gray vending machines with privacy curtains. Robert joined the line of kids waiting to vote, but everyone insisted that he cut ahead, so he ended up having the first turn. When he emerged from the booth, his classmates cheered.

Robert liked the attention more than he expected. Everyone was being so nice to him. At lunch, kids were sharing their desserts, plying him with brownies and Twizzlers. They'd seen the attack firsthand, but they all wanted Robert to tell the story of the giant bird, and he never got tired of repeating it.

Glenn was already predicting a landslide victory. "They're not announcing the winners until the Halloween dance, but I think you can start celebrating—"

"The dance!" Robert exclaimed. "I forgot all about it. I never bought tickets. I don't even have a costume."

"I'll take care of it," Glenn said. "I still owe you a few bucks anyway."

This was one of his favorite jokes. In truth, Glenn owed Robert close to five hundred dollars. For most of the fifth and sixth grade, when Glenn was still the biggest bully in Dunwich, he had forced Robert to pay a daily one-dollar "dweeb tax." But after Robert saved Glenn from a giant squid-monster, Glenn promised to repay the tax, all five hundred dollars' worth, in tiny payments every week.

Later that evening, Glenn showed up at Robert's house with two tickets to the Halloween dance and a canvas duffel bag full of army and navy gear. His father and brothers were all active or ex-military and their house was full of government-issue apparel: camo fatigues, field jackets, flak vests, combat boots. Glenn brought all of it.

"You want to go as soldiers?" Robert asked.

"Warren said we're at war," Glenn explained. "I figured we might as well dress like it."

CHAPTER

SIXTEEN

It was already dark when the boys left the house, and rain was coming down in sheets. The moment they stepped outside, they were completely drenched. They ran the entire eight blocks to Lovecraft Middle School. By the time they arrived, the dance was already under way; most of their teachers and classmates were already inside.

The front door was blocked by a hump-backed witch with green skin and long, stringy black hair. She carried a broom with a Home Depot bar-code sticker on its handle.

"Hello, my pretties!" she cackled. "Welcome to my haunted mansion! You must be Robert Arthur and

Glenn Torkells!"

Robert wondered how she knew his name. The witch didn't look like any of his teachers, and she was too old to be a student. He held out his ticket.

"I don't need your ticket," the witch explained. "I just need a big kiss." She turned and offered her cheek. It was green and crusty and disgusting.

"I don't think so," Robert said.

The witch didn't move. "I'm still waiting, dearie."

"I won't."

She grabbed his arm. "You will!"

Robert leapt backward. "Let go!"

"Sweetie, it's *me*." The witch dropped the cheese-ball voice and lifted the black hair away from her face. "It's *Mom*."

Glenn laughed hysterically. "Holy cow, Mrs. Arthur, that's really you?"

His mother straightened her back and grinned. "Isn't it cool? I bought the wig at a flea market. Five dollars."

"Yeah, real cool," Robert sighed. After being attacked by a giant snake and a shrieking harpy in the same week, Halloween scares weren't as funny as they used to be. "Can we go inside now? I'm soaked."

"Brace yourselves," Mrs. Arthur warned. "Because I have something really special to show you."

With a dramatic flourish, she stepped aside, allowing the boys to enter the lobby. The walls were draped with black velvet. Pipe-cleaner spiders dangled from the ceiling. The floor was covered with green Astroturf and Styrofoam tombstones. And looming in the distance was a familiar four-story mansion.

Somehow, Robert found himself standing outside Tillinghast Mansion.

"What's going on?" he asked.

"Isn't it incredible?" his mother whispered.

"Where's the gate? How did we get here?"

"Gate? What are you talking about?"

Glenn crossed the Astroturf, approaching the house, and tapped the wall with his knuckle. It made a dull, hollow noise. "It's cardboard," he said. "It's fake."

"Of course it's fake," Mrs. Arthur said, "but doesn't it look realistic? Isn't the detail amazing? The Parents

Association has been working on it for weeks."

It was an enormous model of Tillinghast, scaled down to fit into the school's lobby, with its most distinctive architectural features painted on layers of flat cardboard.

"Wow," Glen whispered.

"Here's the best part." Mrs. Arthur pushed open the cardboard front door and led them into a replica of Tillinghast's entrance hall, complete with a cardboard staircase, a cardboard fireplace, a cardboard chandelier, even cardboard reproductions of the tapestries.

Tables of food and drink were arranged on both sides of the room. Mrs. Arthur took great delight in pointing out all of what she called the dreadfully tasty treats.

"Maybe you'd like some fresh eyeballs?" she asked, then lowered her voice to a confidential whisper. "They're just peeled grapes."

"I know," Robert said.

"Or how about some Witch's Brew?" she cackled. "No, seriously, it's just lemonade with gummy worms."

"Mom, I get it," Robert said.

She frowned. "You don't seem very impressed."

"Whose idea was this? The staircase, the fireplace, the tapestries?"

"Oh, Mr. Price thought of everything. Sarah and Sylvia's father. He heads the Parents Association and he designed the whole thing. Here he comes now."

To anyone else at the dance, it might seem like Mr. Price wasn't in costume. He was dressed for work at his law firm, in a charcoal three-button suit with a crisp white shirt and burgundy tie. But Robert and Glenn understood that Mr. Price *was* the costume—that beneath the fancy tailoring and suntanned skin lurked another of Tillinghast's horrific monsters.

"That's a good disguise," Glenn said.

"You haven't seen the best part," Mrs. Arthur said. "Go on, Bill, show him."

Mr. Price smiled, revealing a pair of cheap plastic vampire fangs. "Watch out! I'm a blood-sucking lawyer!"

"Isn't that funny?" Mrs. Arthur laughed. "I think it's so original."

Sarah and Sylvia followed their father into the hall; they were dressed in matching pink princess gowns and pointy hats. The girls hurried toward Robert and Glenn holding paper towels from the restroom.

"You poor things," Sarah said. "You're dripping wet!"

"Maybe you'd like to sit by the fire," Sylvia suggested. "You'll be warm and toasty in no time."

"Oh, that's cute!" Mrs. Arthur said.

Robert refused the towels. "We're okay."

"Yeah," Glenn said. "We'll dry off at the dance. But you should come with us, Mrs. Arthur. I'm sure they need chaperones inside."

Mr. Price shook his head. "We need her at the front door. In case any more latecomers show up." He spoke like a good lawyer, with so much conviction and authority that no one dared question his decision. "But don't worry, Mrs. Arthur, I'm happy to keep you company."

"Please," she said, laughing, "call me Mary."

Robert didn't like the idea of leaving his mother

in Tillinghast Mansion, even if it was a fake replica of Tillinghast Mansion, and especially not with a monster disguised as Mr. Price. But she was already hurrying him toward the dance. "Go on, kids, have fun! I want to see some fancy footwork out there!"

"Thanks, Mrs. Arthur!" Sarah said.

"You're the best!" Sylvia exclaimed.

Glenn pushed open the door and they entered the gymnasium. It was decorated like the lobby, filled with fake cobwebs and glowing jack-o'-lanterns and fog machines pumping misty vapors across the empty dance floor. Most kids were loitering on the sidelines, a bunch of zombies and pirates and vampires. At the far end of the gym was a small stage where a high-school student played DJ, blasting pop music over giant speakers.

Sarah and Sylvia stepped boldly to the center of the dance floor, waving their arms and shaking their hips.

"Let's get this party started!" Sarah exclaimed.

"Woooooo!" Sylvia said. "Go, Lovecraft!"

They were dancing alone—but only for a moment. Soon the zombies and pirates and vampires stepped forward to join them, as if drawn to the Price sisters by some kind of powerful magnetic force. Within minutes, the dance floor was packed.

"It's like they have everyone under a spell," Robert observed. "Do you think Tillinghast gave them special powers?"

Glenn shook his head. "They're just popular, that's all. They don't need any other powers."

The boys found Karina sitting alone at the top of the bleachers. She wore a wispy white gown and a ring of flowers in her hair. Draped around her shoulders was a length of metal chain.

"What are you supposed to be?" Glenn asked.

"I'm a ghooooost," Karina moaned, rattling the chain with both hands. "I'm trapped for eeeeeternity in a middle schooooool. Help meeeeee."

Robert laughed. "You need to work on your acting."

They sat down and Robert unzipped the pocket of his flak vest. Pip and Squeak climbed out and sat beside him. It was eight-thirty and the election results wouldn't be announced until nine o'clock. They passed

the time trying to identify teachers and faculty, all of
whom were in costume. Mr. Loomis was dressed as
Abraham Lincoln, with a black overcoat, fake beard, and
tall stovepipe hat. Coach Glandis had come as Michael
Jackson, sporting a red leather jacket and a single white

sequined glove. And Ms. Lavinia was dressed as a mermaid, complete with a shimmering turquoise gown and ruffled tail fin. She was filling a cup at the punch bowl when she was approached by a man in a wet suit, diving helmet, and swim fins. She recognized him at once, dropped her cup, and pulled him into an embrace.

"Is that who I think it is?" Glenn asked.

It was Warren Lavinia, Robert realized. *Of course.* Halloween was the one time of year when Ms. Lavinia's husband could come into Lovecraft Middle School wearing a mask without anyone getting suspicious. He had promised his wife they would be together soon, and he had kept his word.

The lights in the gymnasium dimmed, the music switched to a slow song, and the Lavinias drifted onto the dance floor. All around them, boys and girls were pairing up. Robert scratched the back of his neck. Karina crossed her legs and then uncrossed them.

Glenn elbowed Robert in the ribs. "You should go dance."

"I don't feel like it."

"Are you chicken?"

"I'm not chicken, I just don't feel like it."

"Any girl in the seventh grade would dance with you tonight," Glenn said. "You just have to ask. You're a hero now. You should be down there with the cool kids."

"I'm happy here."

"What about Lynn Scott? She's cute."

"I don't think so."

Glenn was incredulous. "You don't think Lynn's cute? She's gorgeous! Look at her hula costume. Look at those shells!"

"I don't want to dance with her."

"Why not?"

"Because I don't."

"Why not?"

"Will you leave him alone?" Karina snapped. "He says he's happy sitting here. Quit bugging him."

Glenn threw up his hands, exasperated. "I'm just trying to take his mind off the election. He looks nervous."

Robert confessed he was worried about his mother. "I don't like her being alone out there with Mr. Price. I'm afraid something bad is going to happen."

"Glenn and I will go check on her," Karina offered. "We'll make sure she's okay. You wait here in case they announce the results."

They left and Robert was glad he didn't have to talk about dancing anymore. He had no interest in dancing with any of the girls in seventh grade, except maybe Karina. But how do you dance with a girl who isn't really there? How do you hold hands with a ghost?

He was still pondering these questions when he noticed Howard Mergler ascending the bleacher stairs. Each step required a tremendous amount of effort. He was using his forearm crutches like climbing poles, as if he was scaling Mount Everest.

"Howard!" Robert called. "You want me to come down?"

"I can make it," he called back. "Just give me a second."

More than a few minutes passed before Howard

finally reached the summit of the bleachers. Robert couldn't make sense of his costume; he wore a wild white wig and bushy white mustache that made him look like an old man.

Then Robert noticed Howard's T-shirt. It read: $E=mc^2$.

"You're Albert Einstein," he said.

Howard nodded. "The father of modern physics. You're the first person to recognize me. Well done."

"How do you like the dance?"

"I'm not much of a dancer," Howard said. "I'm only here for the election results."

Robert laughed. "Me, too."

"Well, let me congratulate you ahead of time," Howard said, shaking his hand. "If I have to lose to someone, I'm glad it's you instead of Sarah Price."

Robert was confused. "You don't know that you've lost."

Howard laughed. "Yes, I do. I should have known it was pointless to try. People like me never get to be president."

"How do you mean?"

He gestured to his legs. "Franklin Roosevelt was the last person to pull it off. He was stuck in a wheelchair and voters still elected him president of the United States. But that was before TV, before the Internet. These days it's all about image."

Robert admitted that it seemed unfair.

"No one said life is fair," Howard said. "But I'll be fine. Maybe I'll try out for Handwriting Club. I hear they're always looking for new members." He shrugged. "Anyhow, I just wanted to say congratulations."

Howard hobbled down the steps, returning to the dance floor to await the election results. Robert decided the whole student council election was stupid. Either Sarah would win because she was pretty and popular, or Robert would win because he hit a giant bird with a music stand. Neither outcome was right— and the one candidate with good ideas didn't stand a chance.

But there was no time to dwell on the injustice of it all.

Glenn was running back to the bleachers. He looked scared, and Glenn didn't frighten easily. Something had to be very wrong.

"It's your mother," he said. "She's gone."

CHAPTER
SEVENTEEN

As they hurried across the dance floor, pushing past all of the vampires and zombies, Glenn explained that he and Karina had already searched outside around the school. "Mr. Price said he needed her to wait outside for latecomers, remember?" he said. "But there's no sign of her anywhere. She's disappeared."

"Where's Karina?"

"Checking the cafeteria. I want to check inside the haunted house."

On the far side of the gym, Mr. Loomis climbed the steps to the stage and tapped the microphone a few times.

"Excuse me, everyone!" he called. "We'll be announcing the winners of the election in just a few minutes. So please, let's all gather in the gymnasium. Everyone come inside, please, all right?"

Robert and Glenn ignored him. There was no time to waste. As their classmates moved toward the stage, the two boys walked in the opposite direction. They pushed open the exit door of the gymnasium and returned to the entrance hall of the fake Tillinghast Mansion.

There was no sign of Mrs. Arthur—but they did find Sarah and Sylvia Price, still dressed in their princess costumes, standing beside the table of pretzels and potato chips and fake eyeballs.

"Where's my mother?" Robert demanded.

"We gave you an extraordinary opportunity," Sarah growled. "You could have surrendered your vessels and served with honor. Now we're going to take them by force!"

The door to the gymnasium slammed shut, and Robert heard the lock click into place. The room was extremely cold. Somehow the tapestry depicting a vortex had transformed into a real vortex, a real gate, rimmed with frost and venting frigid air.

"We won't go," Robert said.

"It's not your choice," Sarah answered.

With extraordinary force and agility, she grabbed Robert's arm and twisted it behind his back, shooting pain up his shoulders until he collapsed to his knees. "There, there," she said. "Stand up, Robert. Be a good little boy and I won't hurt you again."

Glenn tried pushing past Sylvia to no avail. She may have looked like a thirteen-year-old girl, but her strength, speed, and reflexes were superhuman. She flipped Glenn onto his back and knelt on his chest, pinning him to the floor. "Try that again and I'll claw your eyes out," she warned. "We don't need your inferior mammalian vision. Just your hair, muscle, and skin!"

Sarah shoved Robert toward the vortex.

"The spell!" Glenn exclaimed. "Use Warren's spell!"

Of course! The words sprang to his lips: "*K'yaloh f'ah Zhenz'koh.*" Robert sputtered the incantation three times while the Price sisters just laughed.

"It doesn't work twice, you idiot," Sarah said. "You've already brought Zhenz'koh into your world, so you can't summon her again."

She shoved him forward another step. With his free hand, Robert reached for anything that might be used as a weapon. He grabbed a bowl of pretzels and flung it at Sylvia. The container clanged off her head and tumbled to the floor, spilling salty snacks everywhere.

Sylvia seemed amused. "You can't harm us," she explained. "We descend from an ancient race of superior life forms. Look what I can do." She grabbed a handful of Glenn's hair, pulling him off the floor and tossing him upside-down, like a child's rag doll. Glenn hit the floor hard and groaned. He was helpless.

Sarah shoved Robert forward yet another step. Now he could feel the force of the vortex, drawing him into its vacuum. He was inches away from spending eternity in a ceramic jar. One more step and it would all be over.

Desperate, he grabbed a cup of Witch's Brew from

the table and tossed it in Sarah's face, hoping it might slow her for just a moment. One last second on earth before an eternity of torment.

To his astonishment, Sarah shrieked.

She released her grip on Robert and stumbled backward, clutching her face. Her skin was venting tiny plumes of gray smoke, as if it had somehow been ignited.

"Nooo!" Sylvia bellowed.

There was no time to think about what was happening or why. Robert grabbed the bowl of Witch's Brew and dumped it over Sylvia's head. She ducked but wasn't fast enough. She fell to the floor, howling with rage.

Robert spotted a few slices of lemon at the bottom of the punch bowl—and suddenly he understood what was going on. His mother had made the Witch's Brew; she described the recipe as plain old lemonade with gummy worms.

It was, in other words, a two-gallon vat of citric acid—the same substance Warren had used to dissolve the hermit crabs and reveal the cthulhus.

Robert reached under Glenn's shoulders, lifting him up. "Are you okay?"

"I think so," Glenn said, still groggy. "What's happening?"

Sarah and Sylvia were writhing on the floor, their skin molting from their bodies as Robert and Glenn watched in horror. They were reacting to the acid just as the hermit crab had in Warren's laboratory—except their decomposition was a thousand times more disgusting. Skin melted down, peeling off in pink, gooey slabs. The smell was appalling. What remained of their bodies was green, scaled, slimy, and only vaguely human. Instead of legs, each beast ended in long, slithering tails. Instead of hair, their heads were crowned with a tangle of live snakes.

Robert and Glenn bolted for the front exit—the door leading to the front of the school—but the snake-sisters were faster, cracking their massive tails across the room and blocking the way. "*Fai throdog ky'osiss!*" they chanted together. "*Fai throdog ky'osiss!*"

"What are they doing?" Glenn asked. "What does that mean?"

"I don't know," Robert said.

"*Fai throdog ky'osiss! Fai throdog ky'osiss!*" As the sisters continued their chant, their hideous hair-snakes swayed to its rhythm, hissing along with every "*ky'osiss.*"

The gate was spinning faster; its black vortex was accelerating. One of the snakesisters lashed her tail at Robert, and it tethered around his waist like a bullwhip. "You're coming with usssss!" she hissed. "Now that you've destroyed our vessssssels, Master will insisssst on replacements!"

The other serpent-beast snapped her tail around Glenn's legs, knocking him off balance. He fell to the floor, unable to stand. The vortex spun faster and faster, creating a powerful vacuum. Everything that wasn't bolted down—the party streamers, the pretzel bowl, the cardboard chandelier, the melted vessels, the puddles of skin and slime and ooze—all of it was slurped up into the vortex.

Robert hooked one arm around a handrail mounted to the wall. Glenn wasn't close enough to reach it, so he grabbed Robert's free hand instead. The snakesisters slithered toward the gate, pulling the boys with their tails, but Glenn held fast to Robert and Robert held tight to the railing.

He knew he wouldn't last long. Their only hope was for someone in the gymnasium to unlock the door and come to their rescue.

"Help!" Robert shouted.

"Help us!" Glenn screamed. "Somebody! Please!"

They hollered and yelled, but the gymnasium was too noisy; no one could hear them over the music. Except—

"Robert Arthur? Is that you?"

A lone voice on the other side of the door.

It was Mr. Loomis!

"We're getting ready to announce the winners," he explained. "What are you doing in there?" The door rattled in its frame as Mr. Loomis tried to open it. "And why is this door locked?"

"We're trapped!" Robert yelled back. "Do you have a key?"

"I don't, but I could find a custodian," he proposed. "Why don't you boys sit tight for a few minutes? I'll see what I can do . . ."

Robert didn't have a few minutes. The snake-sisters were pulling harder on his legs. His fingers were slipping off the railing. He realized that no amount of physical strength would help him now. He was going to spend eternity in a ceramic jar, after all. Unless—

Something on the wall caught his attention.

Robert had an idea.

"Grab my leg!" he told Glenn.

"Are you crazy?"

"I need my other hand! Hurry!"

Robert knew he would only have one chance. With Glenn and a snakesister pulling on his legs, the force would be overwhelming; he wouldn't last more than a second. As soon as Glenn released his hand, Robert lunged forward, reaching for the wall.

And pulled the handle of the fire alarm.

The siren was instantaneous and deafening. Lovecraft's state-of-the-art fire safety system immediately unlocked every door in the school, so that no student would be trapped in the blaze. The snakesisters bellowed in frustration. They released their grip and then dove into the vortex, which promptly closed and vanished, leaving just a faint ring of frost on the cardboard tapestry.

Robert and Glenn collapsed to the floor.

An instant later, the door to the gym crashed open and a group of adults led by Principal Slater came charging in. "Where's the fire?" she asked.

"It's a false alarm," Robert said.

Principal Slater punched a code into the alarm panel and the siren stopped abruptly. There was no trace of the sunny, friendly, former soap-opera actress in her expression. Now she simply looked furious.

"Which one of you did this?" she asked. "And what's that awful stench? It smells disgusting in here!"

"I'll explain later," Robert said. "I need to find my mom."

Mrs. Arthur was standing behind Principal Slater, along with Mr. Price and Mr. Loomis. "I'm right here," she said. "I was helping in the cafeteria when this girl in a ghost costume said you were looking for me. What the heck is going on?"

Thank you, Karina, Robert thought.

"Pulling a fire alarm is a serious criminal offense," Principal Slater said. "Now I'm going to ask my question one more time, and I want an answer. Who did this?"

Robert said, "It was—"

"Sarah and Sylvia," Glenn interrupted.

"Impossible!" Mr. Price shouted, pushing past the other adults to look Glenn in the eyes. "You know that's a lie! My daughters would never pull a false alarm!"

"Go ahead and ask them," Glenn shrugged. "If you can find them."

Mr. Price glanced around the room and his gaze settled on the faint outline of white frost where the vortex used to be. In an instant he seemed to understand that something had gone terribly wrong.

"Where are they?"

"I think they went home," Robert said.

Glenn nodded. "They had some lemonade and it made them a little jumpy. Too much sugar, I guess. I don't think they're coming back."

Mr. Loomis looked exasperated. "But I need to announce the winners! Everyone's waiting to hear the results! Sarah needs to be here!"

Mr. Price continued staring at the tapestry until the white frost vanished, and then he turned away in disgust. "I need to make an announcement of my own," he said. "I'm afraid I have some very bad news."

CHAPTER

EIGHTEEN

The dance resumed quickly after the false alarm, but at precisely nine twenty-seven p.m., Mr. Loomis climbed the steps of the stage and tapped on the microphone, calling once again for everyone's attention. He was still wearing the fake beard and stovepipe hat, and he spoke in his deepest and most reverent voice. "Four score and seven minutes ago," he intoned, "we began the first dance in the history of Lovecraft Middle School. And now we shall make history again—by revealing the name of our first student council president!"

Kids and teachers clapped and cheered. Robert stood at the edge of the audience, accompanied by

Glenn and Karina (and Pip and Squeak, who were resting comfortably in the pocket of his flak vest). It was a weird feeling: just a few short minutes ago, he was nearly dragged into a nightmarish alternate universe by a pair of hideous snakesisters. Now he was surrounded by all his classmates and sipping root beer from a paper cup, as if life was perfectly normal.

"But before I announce the winner," Mr. Loomis continued, "I'm afraid I have some unfortunate news. I just spoke with Mr. Price, the wonderful leader of our Parents Association, and he tells me that his daughters Sarah and Sylvia are moving to the United Kingdom, effective immediately, to study abroad with their extended families. We will miss them dearly, and we wish them all the best."

The other students gasped, and Mr. Loomis allowed a few moments of silence before proceeding. "Of course, Sarah was a candidate in today's student council election, and she did receive one hundred and eight votes. But I'm pleased to announce that her departure will not change the results, because the first-place candidate, garnering one hundred and twelve votes, is Robert Arthur!"

The gymnasium erupted with cheers and applause and birdcalls. Glenn whooped his approval and started his chant again—"Let's GO, Rob-ERT!"—and this time the other students all joined in. "Let's GO, Rob-ERT!"

He couldn't believe it. He had won! In the span of a single day, he'd gone from being a total nobody to the most popular kid in school.

"You better get up there," Karina whispered. "People are waiting."

As Robert climbed the steps of the stage, he saw his mother standing at the back of the gym, dabbing at her eyes with a tissue. She was so proud of him. All his classmates were clapping. Even Howard Mergler was leaning against a wall so that his hands were free to applaud.

"Congratulations, Robert," Mr. Loomis said, shaking his hand and giving him the microphone. "Would you like to say a few words?"

Just twelve hours earlier Robert had been onstage at the student council debate, and that had been enough public speaking to last him all year. Still, there was something important he needed to say. He waved his hands, calling for silence.

"I'd like to thank everyone who voted for me. Yesterday, I don't think any of you knew my name. Today, because I hit a bird with a music stand, I'm famous."

The crowd went nuts, and more birdcalls erupted from the audience. Two goofy boys ran in circles, flapping their arms, pretending to be hawks or eagles.

"But I realized something tonight," Robert continued. "The best candidate for president isn't the guy who hits a bird with a music stand. And it's not the girl who promises free cupcakes every Friday. It's the person with real ideas for improving this school. And that's not me."

Mr. Loomis was flabbergasted. "You don't *want* the position?"

"I don't deserve it," Robert said. "But I think there's

a person on the ballot who does."

As Robert left the stage, the audience was silent. Mr. Loomis returned to the podium and fumbled through his notes. "This is completely unprecedented," he said. "With Mr. Arthur declining the position and Miss Price moving to the United Kingdom—I suppose the winner is the third-place candidate. Ladies and gentlemen, put your hands together for the new student council president of Lovecraft Middle School, Howard Mergler!"

CHAPTER

NINETEEN

"That was a real dumb idea," Glenn muttered.

"Excuse me?" Robert asked.

The dance was nearly over, and Robert was back in the bleachers with his best friends.

"We worked all week to win this election. We could have been kings of the seventh grade! But now Howard Mergler will be calling the shots." Glenn shook his head, disgusted. "Dumb idea."

"It was the right thing to do," Karina said. "I'm proud of him."

"*I'm proud of him,*" Glenn repeated in a high falsetto. "Give me a break." The music switched to a slow song—one last dance before the night was over—and the boys and girls were pairing up again. "Lynn Scott's never going to dance with you now."

Karina sighed. "Here we go again."

"I'm not interested in Lynn Scott," Robert insisted. "She's beautiful!"

"If you like her so much, why don't *you* dance with her?"

Glenn shrugged. "I already have a date."

He was holding Pip and Squeak in his lap. He raised their forepaws, waving them back and forth in time to the music, and the rats chattered happily, enjoying the attention.

"I'm happy right here," Robert said. "I don't need to dance with anyone."

"Me, neither," Karina said, sitting back and enjoying the music. "I wish we could stay here all weekend."

When the last song ended and the lights came up, the Lavinias climbed the bleachers to congratulate Robert on his victory.

"Well done, young man," Warren said.

"We're very proud of you," Ms. Lavinia said. "You

showed a lot of strength tonight."

Robert shrugged. "The lemonade did most of the work. It melted their skin right off."

"I'm talking about the election. Giving the position to Howard Mergler."

Glenn rolled his eyes. "Such a dumb idea."

"It was the right move," Ms. Lavinia said, "but I'm sure it wasn't an easy move to make."

"I have bigger responsibilities now," Robert said.

"You sure do," Warren said, rubbing his hands together. "We've got a huge fight ahead of us. Tonight was just the warm-up. I'm developing a new weapon "

Ms. Lavinia rested a gentle hand on the back of his diving helmet, interrupting him. "They've had enough fun for one night," she said. "We can talk on Monday."

"Come to the lighthouse!" Warren told them. "My cthulhus are growing. The aquarium won't hold them much longer. We need a plan—"

"Monday," Ms. Lavinia repeated, taking Warren's gloved hand and leading him away. "Enjoy your weekend."

Karina stood up. "I should go, too. The janitors will be locking up, and I'll need a place to hide."

Robert remembered what Karina had said about long, lonely weekends at Lovecraft Middle School. "Do they ever unlock the doors on Saturday or Sunday? I could visit."

She shook her head. "There's no way in or out. I'm on my own until Monday morning."

As she turned to leave, Pip and Squeak leapt out of Glenn's lap and followed her, pacing in circles around her ankles, sniffing her shoes. "What do they want?" she asked.

Robert studied them carefully. His pets were acting so peculiar—like they were intent on going home with Karina instead of him. "Call me crazy," he said, "but I think they're asking if they can sleep over."

Karina grinned. "Here? Really? The whole weekend?" Pip and Squeak nodded their heads. "Oh my gosh, Robert, is that cool with you?"

"Sure," he said. "You'll need to feed them, but I'm sure there's stuff in the cafeteria. They eat almost anything."

"This is awesome!" Karina exclaimed. "I'll take great care of them, I promise, and you'll have them back first thing Monday morning." She looked down at the rats. "We are going to have so much fun together! Wait until you see the teacher's lounge! They have the best snacks!"

Pip squeaked, Squeak chattered happily, and Karina marched them out of the gymnasium.

By this time, most of the other students had already left. Robert and Glenn found Mrs. Arthur in the lobby, taking down the decorations and placing them in a large cardboard box. It was filled to the brim with skulls, severed hands, and rubber rats.

"The school doesn't want them, so I thought we'd bring them home," she explained. "I know how much you boys love Halloween."

Robert could remember when Halloween was his favorite holiday. He used to love all the blood and guts and crazy creature costumes. Now it didn't seem quite so fun anymore. But there was no point in spoiling the tradition.

"Cool," he said. "We can decorate tomorrow, before the trick-or-treaters start coming around."

"And I'll make hot apple cider," Mrs. Arthur said. "Glenn, I hope you'll join us."

"Sure," he said. "I'll bring some gummy worms."

The boys waited outside the main entrance with the box of decorations while Mrs. Arthur went to get the car. It was late, and the parking lot was eerily empty. Robert heard the familiar noise of shuffling feet and clanking metal in the distance.

He turned to see Howard Mergler limping along on his forearm crutches. He was still wearing his $E=mc^2$ T-shirt but had ditched the rest of the Einstein costume.

"Hi, guys," he called.

"Hey, Mr. President," Robert said. "You need a ride?"

He shook his head. "No, thanks. I'll manage."

"You're sure?" It was nearly eleven o'clock, and Howard lived more than a mile across town. At the rate he crept along, he'd be lucky to get home before dawn.

"I just came over to say thank you."

"You don't have to thank me," Robert said. "You deserved to win. You're going to make a terrific president."

Howard stood up straight, full of pride. "I'll do my best. I have so many plans for our class. And I appreciate your giving me the opportunity. That was really generous of you."

"My pleasure," Robert said. "Good luck."

"I just want to be clear that this doesn't change things for Master. You destroyed two vessels tonight and he's very unhappy."

Robert blinked. "What?"

"This election was meant to be a contest between me and Sarah. Brains versus beauty. A win for Master, either way. You came along and nearly ruined the whole plan." Howard shook his head sadly. "When I lead our classmates into Tillinghast Mansion, I'm afraid you boys will suffer the worst."

Headlights flashed over the main entrance. Mrs. Arthur was driving out of the parking lot and heading toward them. Howard reached down, unstrapping the heavy orthotic braces that circled his knees. Then he tossed the braces into the nearest trash can and added the crutches as well. Finally he stood up straight on his own two feet.

"You can walk?" Robert asked.

"Please," Howard sneered. "Walking is for mammals."

He turned and sprinted across the athletic field, faster than was humanly possible. In an instant he was just a shadow on the horizon—the shadow of Lovecraft Middle School's new student council president, beating his enormous wings and rising above the treetops, soaring through the moonlit sky.

Robert stared after him.

Glenn snorted. "Told you it was a dumb idea."

About the Author

Charles Gilman is an alias of Jason Rekulak, an editor who lives in Philadelphia with his wife, Julie, and their children Sam and Anna. When he's not dreaming up new tales of Lovecraft Middle School, he's biking along the fetid banks of the Schuylkill River, in search of two-headed rats and other horrific beasts.

About the Illustrator

From an early age, Eugene Smith dreamed of drawing monsters, mayhem, and madness. Today, he is living the dream in Chicago, Illinois, where he resides with his wife, Mary, and their daughters Audrey and Vivienne.

Monstrous Thanks

Doogie Horner, John McGurk, Jane Morley, Mary Ellen Wilson, Jen Adams, David Borgenicht, Brett Cohen, Nicole De Jackmo, Eric Smith, Moneka Hewlett, Ron Fladwood, Evangeline Young, Audrey Coughenour, Jonathan Pushnik, Mike Russell, Ed and Heidi Milano, Roseann Rekulak, Julie Scott, and Mary Flack.